Dr. Alexander Gorjan,

leading scientist of a small Communist country, is a man with a hearty appetite for work, women, and wine. Ostensibly he is in England for the Andover Lecture of the Imperial Circle of Scientists. But actually he is there for quite another reason. A far more sinister reason.

Dr. Gorjan proves a most troublesome guest to Colonel Charles Russell of Britain's Security Executive. Especially when he provokes the interest of two foreign powers—one friend and one foe.

Even so, Russell is more than willing to abide by the rules. He remains an interested but non-active participant in the diplomatic chess game . . . until a midnight attempt on the life of the scientist threatens to turn a delicate situation into an international crisis. Then the urbane Security officer throws away the rules of the game and plays it rough. Very rough indeed.

"HAGGARD . . . WRITES WITH SOPHISTI-CATION AND AUTHORITY OF PLOYS AND COUNTER-PLOYS, WHETHER THEY ARE MADE IN BEDROOMS OR IN WHITE-HALL." —*Chicago Tribune*

"*The Antagonists* IS AS LIVELY AND ACTION-FILLED A SAGA OF INTERNATION-AL INTRIGUE AS ANY READER COULD HOPE FOR." —*Houston Chronicle*

William Haggard

The
ANTAGONISTS

A SIGNET BOOK
published by The New American Library

Published as a SIGNET BOOK
by arrangement with Ives Washburn, Inc.,
who have authorized this softcover edition.
A hardcover edition is available from Ives Washburn, Inc.

FIRST PRINTING, AUGUST, 1965

SIGNET TRADEMARK REG. U.S. PAT. OFF. AND FOREIGN COUNTRIES
REGISTERED TRADEMARK—MARCA REGISTRADA
HECHO EN CHICAGO, U.S.A.

SIGNET BOOKS are published by
The New American Library, Inc.
1301 Avenue of the Americas, New York, New York 10022

PRINTED IN THE UNITED STATES OF AMERICA

CHAPTER 1

The Ilyushin was half an hour late already, and the pilot had come back to tell Gorjan that now there would be more delay. He wasn't pleased. It was a scheduled flight, but he was Alexander Gorjan, and a compartment had been screened off for him—four first-class seats. He nodded at the pilot but did not speak. It was better to keep his temper. His head had begun to hurt again and he knew what that meant. It would hurt for two days at least, increasing agony, then suddenly it would be gone again. Or that was what had happened so far. And in a matter of an hour or so he would be giving a formal lecture to the Imperial Circle of Scientists.

He hadn't wanted to come but the President had insisted. The Andover Lecture at the Imperial Circle was a world occasion in the world of science; it had enormous prestige and the country could do with it. The President had almost pleaded, and that wasn't something he did often. He knew Gorjan hadn't been well of late but he would send a doctor with him. Alex Gorjan had declined the doctor.

Now he was wishing he hadn't. His head ached intolerably, forehead and neck too. With a feeling he knew was fear he looked down at his hands. Almost imperceptibly they had begun to twitch again. The reflex movement, uncontrolled, disgusted him.

No, he shouldn't have come. He'd been working too hard, but he was too much a realist to blame the fact. Men didn't have breakdowns through overwork alone, or his sort of man didn't. But they might if they burnt it at both ends, they might if they mixed their drinks, made love to too many women. He was fond of drink, he always had been, and Sonia in particular had been intolerably beautiful. His smile was small but it wasn't dissatisfied. Sonia would remember him.

He put out his hand and pulled the curtain, looking at the aircraft's stuffily Edwardian decoration. The Confederate Republic couldn't really afford the Ilyushin, but it had been offered by a neighbour on terms which had seemed generous but in practice had disclosed themselves as shamelessly usurious. Gorjan smiled sourly. Which ought to have been expected with that particular neighbour. Alexander Gorjan detested them.

He tugged at the curtain, flinching as his head moved. Outside the porthole was a cotton-wool sea of cloud: somewhere below was England. He hadn't seen it for fifteen years. He had enjoyed his time at Cambridge; he had even liked the English. Their hypocrisy hadn't troubled him, only their ignorance that they were hypocrites. But that you got used to, and undeniably Cambridge had been hospitable. It would be strange to see it again after this ridiculous meeting had been dealt with. He had a full week's programme and naturally Cambridge was on it. So for that matter was a place called Oxford. A good Cambridge man, he'd heard of Oxford.

Meanwhile he had to talk to them, these ancient prestigious has-beens. The Circle wasn't science but the graveyard of old scientists. He'd give them a show, though. His English was pretty good still, and he'd been rubbing it up. For Alexander Gorjan that hadn't been difficult. In the Confederate Republic a wish to rub your English up could sometimes bring the police on you with awkward questions about your intentions. But not on Gorjan. He was Alexander Gorjan, well enough known internationally to have been invited to give the Andover Lecture, and he was a good party man which was at least as important. He wasn't an apolitical scientist: on the contrary he was a communist and proud of it. He'd prepared his speech in writing but nobody had asked to see the script. He had unrivalled knowledge in his specialist line and soon he might have something more, but nobody had even hinted that in England he should guard it. He was a good party man in excellent standing.

Privately he put his country first. That too was acceptable in the Confederate Republic.

He rose to his feet suddenly as his head split in two; he gripped the table in front of him, grimacing. When the spasm was over he sat down shakily. The pilot had come back again, looking at him uneasily. His responsibility would end when Gorjan left his aircraft, and it was evident that was something he would be glad of. Gorjan asked shortly: 'Well?'

'Landing in five minutes, sir.'

'That's good.'

They were slipping through the cloud, the flaps falling smoothly, the note of the jets thickening. There was the faintest bump and a long braking run. When they had stopped the steward came to Gorjan first. 'This way, if you please, sir.'

Alexander Gorjan walked along the aircraft to the door. The gangway was already up, but he was surprised to find that it was dark. He had known they were late but not how badly. He opened his mouth and shut it grimly. He had other things to worry him than forty-five minutes' lateness. He must husband his strength, and carefully; he didn't dare risk a useless scene.

He walked down the gangway, a hand on the rail to steady him. The photographers held up cameras and the flashlights nearly blinded him. When he had his sight back he could make out a knot of men. One of them detached himself, shaking hands quickly. 'I'm Jensen,' he said, 'Professor Jensen. We've arranged to waive all formalities. There's a car by the runway and your luggage can follow.' Jensen looked at his watch. 'We'll just about make it.'

'But I ought to change first.' Gorjan had had very precise instructions about his dress. This was White Tie and Decorations. He had brought his decorations, and the fancy dress should have been hired for him in London. He'd sent measurements to his embassy and they'd promised to do the rest. A man from the embassy was to bring everything to the airport, and Gorjan was to have changed there. The schedule had always been tight. Gorjan looked around him, blinking still. His ambassador was coming towards him and another man he recognized as Stevan Starc, First Secretary. Both were in full evening dress but neither carried a bag. The ambassador looked at Gorjan, then looked again, pretending not to. For a second he hesitated, then he said soothingly: 'I'm afraid there'll be a change of plan.'

'But I can't go like this.' Alexander Gorjan was shocked. His country was communist but it respected the formal occasion. He couldn't lecture to the Circle in sports coat and flannel trousers. They'd think he was, well, a communist—their stupid idea of communists.

But Jensen had broken in again. 'We shall all understand,' he said. 'Of course.' His voice was quiet but his manner desperate. The ambassador nodded briefly. His tone changed slightly as he spoke again, and Alex Gorjan could recognize the change.

'You'll have to go as you are. Jensen will explain things.'

Gorjan said furiously: 'He better had.'

They were talking their own language.

The car had slid up to them, and Gorjan and His Excellency got in. There were the driver and another man in front.

. . . That would be the bodyguard. Even in the Confederacy there was always a bodyguard.

In the half light the ambassador looked at Gorjan again. He'd been warned that he wasn't well, but he hadn't been warned of this. Alex Gorjan looked near to death. The ambassador said quietly: 'I'd sleep a bit if I were you. Take a nap.'

'I wish I could.'

It was seven o'clock and the traffic into London moderate. Gorjan shut his eyes and his head dropped instantly. His Excellency had once been a soldier; he knew when to be silent and this was a time for silence. He sat smoking quietly, watching Gorjan's grey face.

. . . He might make it or he might not. Tonight. The rest of the trip was clearly off. They'd been insane to let him come at all, but he was very strong. Tonight perhaps, with luck.

At Burlington House the ambassador nudged Gorjan gently. As his head came up there was a stifled groan.

'We're here.'

They walked through the portico, up the ugly, imposing staircase. For a moment Gorjan rallied. Turning to the ambassador he said: 'Talking first, I believe. Dinner afterwards.'

'That's the arrangement.' His Excellency was pleased with it. Formal talk after dinner he considered uncivilized. This was a concession by the English and one he appreciated. 'Talking first,' he repeated, 'eating afterwards.'

'Could you get me off the eating?'

'Yes, I think I could do that.'

'Then I'll let you know if you have to.'

They walked into a long cold room. It made Gorjan gasp. He came of a frugal race, but nobody in his country stayed freezing unless they had to. And these were rich men. There were a hundred perhaps, on chairs which looked intolerable, facing a dais. On the dais a man was talking, filling in. There were two empty seats, and as Gorjan and the ambassador took them there was a burst of clapping. The speaker sat down and the chairman stood up. He said with a splendid brevity: 'I had intended a speech of welcome. Now you will be spared it. Not that it was necessary, for you all know our guest. His achievements speak better than I do. Your Royal Highness. Your Grace. My lords, ladies and gentlemen.' The chairman raised an arm, an actor's gesture. 'Doctor Alexander Gorjan.'

There was another burst of clapping, then silence as Gorjan rose. He was feeling a little better now. The typescript of his lecture was in his pocket but he had taken great pains with it; he knew it by heart and he was a courteous man. One shouldn't read a lecture unless obliged to. It wasn't polite. He opened his mouth: 'Ladies and gentlemen——'

He swallowed his words, astounded. In the third row of crazy chairs an old, old man had risen. He had a long, lined simian face and thin white hair. And he was talking.

. . . The appalling crisis in which humanity now finds itself. . . .

Gorjan sat down uncertainly. Perhaps he had blundered, perhaps made a fool of himself. The introduction had seemed clear enough, but here was this old monkey nattering.

. . . The moral dilemma which none of us can escape, all races and every creed. The conscience of right-thinking men. . . .

The man beside Gorjan pulled at his sleeve. 'It's Merridew,' he explained. 'Sir William Merridew.'

'Who's Merridew?'

'The Grand Old Man.'

It had sounded like an apology.

'But what's he talking about?'

'The bomb.'

'The bomb! But I'm not an atomic physicist.'

'I know you're not. He seems to have got it wrong, that's all. Nowadays he often does. He's ninety, you see, and more.'

Alex Gorjan was bitterly insulted. Atomic physicists had more than a little depreciated. Once they had been an aristocracy, but now the engineers had taken over. Atomic physicist indeed! He put his hand to his forehead. His moment of relief had gone. In a minute or less the pain would be unbearable.

But the chairman had risen again. 'Sir William's views', he was saying smoothly, 'are well known to all of us. And entitled, if I may say so, to our unqualified respect.' He bowed at Sir William Merridew. 'But on this of all occasions——'

'I will not be silenced.' The Polonius voice, a senile treble, ran up the scale alarmingly, cracked at the top. 'The future of humanity is in our hands, nay——'

Alex Gorjan had risen too. He was in dreadful pain again. He fingered his neck, feeling it where it joined his spine. His head was on his body still: it didn't seem so. He drew a deliberate breath. He had a fine deep chest and a fine deep voice came out of it.

'Silly old bastard. Ignorant clown.'

There was an appalled and appalling silence. The chairman got to 'Gentlemen', but Gorjan pushed him firmly down. He steadied himself with his other hand. The agony was purple now, then red. Through it his voice rang savagely: 'Fascist. Imperialist. Impotent aged pig.'

'Gentlemen, gentlemen, I beg you, I——'

Alexander Gorjan was suddenly terrified. He couldn't see, he was going blind. Sir William Merridew had disappeared, then he was back again, enormous, looming. Gorjan felt on the table, his hands moving urgently. There'd been water in a heavy glass carafe. His hands found it blindly for his eyes were still on Merridew. He hadn't dared move them. He pulled back his arm and for an instant Merridew was huge again. He threw and Sir William fell.

There was immediate pandemonium. Somebody was wiping blood from Sir William Merridew's face. Gorjan didn't see it. He was lying across the table; he was out.

A little earlier Colonel Charles Russell had been walking home from his cosily untidy room in the Security Executive. His day hadn't been more worrying than usual, and in any case he handled worry well. Which meant in Whitehall that when a man shut his office door behind him he could walk unhesitatingly into a different and wholly private world. Most servants of the State could not, or not the ambitious ones. They took work home, they fussed incessantly. Sometimes they made the Honours List, more often they didn't, and mostly they died within a year or two of pensioning. Charles Russell hadn't been knighted but his expectation of life was excellent.

He walked across St. James's Park, sixty but erect still, casually elegant, glancing at the evening paper as he went. . . . So Dr Gorjan's plane had been considerably delayed. Charles Russell knew about Gorjan. It wasn't formally his business to watch the safety of very important visitors, but he would have agreed that one of the charms of work in the Security Executive was that its responsibilities were never defined precisely. A charm and often an advantage too. You paid for it of course, since when something went wrong you were apt to be carpeted by political masters who had forgotten or neglected to inform you of a danger. Colonel Charles Russell smiled. He liked it that way and he paid the price gladly. So the safety of Alexander Gorjan was the responsibility of the Special Branch, and Russell had a high opinion of its competence.

That hadn't prevented his slipping a man of his own into Gorjan's entourage.

He strode on briskly, thinking about Gorjan. Alexander Gorjan was a radar man, which in the context of contemporary anarchy meant an early warning man, and a scientist with an edge in early warning was at least as important as another with a bigger bomb or better rocket. In conditions of nuclear stalemate he could even be his master. But it wasn't only Gorjan's professional reputation which was interesting. Gorjan was a man, an authentic individual. The traditional picture of the international scientist was certainly a stereotype, and in the world of security stereotypes were dangerous oversimplifications. Not that Gorjan could ever have been considered one. Stereotypes be damned! This was a man.

Which, Russell reflected, had been one of his reasons for adding to the precautions which the Special Branch would certainly have taken. The Special Branch was efficient; and since most important visitors could be relied on to stick to a programme as rigid as a seminary's your sleep would be undisturbed. But Gorjan couldn't be relied on to follow a schedule which bored him. Take him to an official dinner—there were several, it seemed—and if the company were tedious Gorjan would turn to the wine. If that were good he would console himself. He was far too hard-headed to behave regrettably, but it might be some stranger's taxi which he casually shared home. Leaving an official car, a Special Branch driver in it, untidily behind him. Or take him to a cocktail party and he wouldn't drink at all. He had the civilized man's contempt for cocktails but an equal eye for a pretty woman. When he saw one, if she liked him, he would take her on to dinner. To wherever she chose. To the Savoy perhaps, which was easy enough, or to some box of a *trattoria* which was not. The lady might not care a damn: the Special Branch shadow would.

Charles Russell's smile broadened. Gorjan was one to play by ear so that was the way he'd play it.

He let himself into his unpretentious flat and turned on the telly. There was a spy serial which he was watching avidly, though he knew that if spying in life had been as neat and well-constructed as this goggle-box thriller he would have been out of a job in a month. He settled with a drink. . . . Now the man in the Shaftesbury Avenue suit was obviously a suspect; he was *intended* to be a suspect, though he mightn't be the right one. The clothes were significant, and the flash cigarette-lighter. Whereas the slow sort of chap with the kindly manner. . . . It was accepted technique and entirely justified. If only life were like it.

When the telephone rang peremptorily Russell looked at his desk. Two instruments stood on it and their notes were a little different. This was the one without a dial. Russell rose resignedly, flicking off the telly. He picked up the receiver.

'Colonel Russell? It's Copeman here, sir.'

'Good evening, Copeman.'

'I hope you're going to think so, sir. I'm speaking from the Imperial Circle. There's been a, well——'

'Tell me.'

The voice on the telephone began to talk quickly. When it had finished Charles Russell said: 'I'd have given two ponies to see it. And afterwards?'

'They handled it pretty slickly, Merridew wasn't seriously hurt. His wife mopped him up and removed him. Gorjan was unconscious but his own people looked after him—his ambassador and another man called Starc. They had an ambulance there in no time. It took him to the Hemmingway Hospital.'

'The Hemmingway, you say? But that's out in the country.'

'If you call Egham country.'

'For the purposes you're paid for it isn't London.' Russell reflected. 'And who was with the ambulance?'

'Male nurse or maybe houseman. Driver. Attendant.'

'Recognize any of them? As friends of ours, I mean.'

'They were strangers to me.'

'Did anyone else board the ambulance?'

'Not that I saw. If you're thinking of our colleagues across the road there was one in the audience. Him I did recognize. And the usual sort of car would have been calling for Gorjan after dinner. That hadn't arrived by then. There was no dinner.'

'But our friend in the audience didn't go near the ambulance?'

'No. I expect he was telephoning—reporting for fresh orders. I'd have done that first myself if I'd had the same masters.'

'I shouldn't be surprised.' Charles Russell's voice was dry. He thought again. 'So our colleagues don't yet know that it's the Hemmingway Hospital?'

'I wouldn't say that, sir. The man we're talking about didn't come near the ambulance, but the attendant made no secret where they were taking Gorjan. A dozen people could have heard him, and for that sort of nervous breakdown the Hemmingway's an obvious bet. In any case, a little quick work on the telephone to the hospitals and——'

'You think our friends will be right behind the ambulance?'

'Maybe not *right* behind. There'll be a flap, of course—there always is on a change of plan. I give them half an hour.'

'Which I won't give anyone. Get over to this Hemmingway at once. Pick another man up if you can.'

'I can.'

'Then do.'

Russell returned to the telly. Somebody was creeping up on someone else, trying to get a shot at him. Charles Russell frowned.

That happened in real life too.

The full style and title of the Hemmingway Hospital was the Hemmingway Hospital for Nervous and Psychiatric Disorders. The word disorders had given the Ministry of Health a month of delicious indecision: diseases versus disorders—it was the sort of thing which an official was happy to minute about indefinitely, and the file had been a good inch thick before the Minister himself, no less, had finally decided for disorders. . . . Poor fellows, poor wretched men and women. You couldn't really say they were *diseased*, now could you? It didn't sound contemporary.

It was a remarkable building, or rather a collection of remarkable buildings. Its heart was a late Victorian mansion in considerable grounds which were now extremely valuable. It had been built by a successful merchant and his taste had been that of his time, a Ruskin Venetian with knobs on. To this Betjeman's delight had been added wings in the glass and concrete manner of a City re-development. Sensitives shuddered, and the establishment cost the taxpayer an annual fortune. There were two opinions whether it was worth it. Psychiatrists, whom it employed extravagantly, were understandably enthusiastic, but family doctors in solid practices had discreet reservations. Doctors who worked in slums would rather not hear about the Hemmingway at all. With a tenth of its annual budget they could have done something useful.

To this monument to a pseudo-science the ambulance had

taken Alexander Gorjan, and for an instant in the small hours he had recovered consciousness. He looked round the little room, trying to focus it. Instinct told him he was in a hospital, but the room was more luxurious than any hospital he'd known. He wasn't in pain and he found he could think. A little and loosely, but he could think. He couldn't remember. There'd been a journey by air from the Confederate Republic, a delay and a lot of pain, then a car and people talking. . . . He gave it up. Clearly they'd drugged him and a good thing too. He'd been right at his limit and he must have gone over it. Otherwise why the hospital? This had happened to him before and he'd always lived. And this seemed a good sort of hospital. There was a nurse on duty, standing by the window, and she had just pulled a curtain back, peeping out from behind it. The curtain was white but the nurse was black.

For an instant his terror returned. Not long ago—he couldn't remember—he had thought he was going blind: now his eyes were again betraying him. He shut them a moment, mastering his fear, then he looked at the nurse again. . . . But of course she was black—Negresses were. He'd heard there were thousands in England. The English had freed their colonies but black men and brown came swarming into England still. Where of course they'd do the dirty work, of course they'd be exploited. He'd been reading about the scandal in the Confederacy's newspapers. Capitalist exploitation. Not that this nurse looked notably exploited. She was a buxom creature, obviously well fed. The girl was really handsome—black but comely. . . . Now where had that bubbled up from? Some book, he supposed, some novel he'd read at Cambridge. He sighed as the drug bit again, and slept.

The nurse hadn't noticed that for a moment he had been conscious. She had been knitting quietly and had risen on an instinct which she wouldn't have admitted. Once, in another life, her mother had taken her out at midnight. They had driven in a jalopy, out of the town, the tarred roads fading into tracks, then into jungle. They had left the car but her mother had known the way. Later a man had met them and her mother had said something in a dialect she didn't understand. She had felt it then, long before the drums began, excitement and something more. The something more was danger.

A month or two later the Baptists had got her. She had gone to the Mission school.

The nurse peeped from the window. In the garden outside it was very dark. And that was all. She shivered but sat down again. She wasn't at ease still.

The grounds behind the Hemmingway, like the heart of the hospital, were laid out in the taste of the 'nineties, a scrubby wood round the perimeter, then, working inwards, a well-attended lawn. After that came a belt of shrubs backing on to a wide gravel terrace. The wall of the house rose sheer from the gravel. Once there had been flower beds to divide the two, now there was only gravel.

Two men were lying in the shrubbery, talking quietly in a foreign tongue. One pointed at a light from a feyly gothic window.

'You think he's in there?'

'There isn't another light. In any case, once we get in——'

'We can't go playing hide and seek—not round a dozen wards.'

'This won't be a ward. The wards will be in the new part. This is for V.I.Ps.'

'Or resident staff?'

The other considered, then shrugged. 'We haven't a better bet,' he said. 'What's more there's that drainpipe. Three floors to go, though. Come.'

They moved across the gravel silently, testing the drainpipe, beginning to climb expertly, and two more men in the shrubbery's shadow nodded approval. They waited till the climbers were half way up, then they moved with an equal silence. At the bottom of the drainpipe Copeman spoke.

'Keep your hands on that pipe.'

The climbers looked down at the two steady guns. One was on each of them.

'You at the top—throw down your gun to me. Move only one hand and throw so I can catch it.'

There was an instant's hesitation.

'You're monkeys on a stick, you know. You're sitters.'

In the glow from the window a pistol glinted suddenly. Copeman caught it neatly, glancing at it and shrugging. He put it in his pocket.

'Now you at the bottom.'

He caught the second pistol too.

'Come down please—gently, gently.'

They came down gently, gently, standing against the wall. They faced the guns silently.

'Now do as you're told. You're coming with us.'

One of the men against the wall said something to the other. Copeman didn't understand him but he caught his tone.

'I wouldn't try anything foolish like a break for it. We've serious weapons here, not what you read about in Sunday-paper supplements. Forty-five calibre. We don't have to go for fancy shooting. We've only to wing you and you won't get up.'

The taller of the two against the wall spoke first. 'And where are you taking us?'

'You'll soon find out.'

CHAPTER 2

Early next morning Colonel Charles Russell was reading a report on the events at the Hemmingway Hospital. It was an interim report, but as far as it went he found it satisfactory. The two men concerned spoke adequate English but their native tongue was the language of the Confederate Republic. So far they hadn't used either much; they hadn't come near to breaking. But they had been identified. Ostensibly they were refugees from the Confederacy and they had entered the country about a month ago both secretly and illegally. When they had immediately disappeared in London. Interrogation was proceeding since it was perfectly safe to hold them. No doubt they would have contacts, but they wouldn't be the kind which would be tempted to risk complaining of a dear friend's absence. A hail of writs was most unlikely.

Russell nodded approvingly. It had often occurred to him that if he had been detailed to do a dirty job in England he would have entered the country openly—the Golden Arrow probably, and making some stupid fuss with Customs, drawing as much attention to himself as possible. If everything went to plan it wouldn't matter, and if he walked into trouble he would rather be detained by the police than secretly held by the Security Executive.

Very much rather.

Russell sat back, considering. He decided that he wouldn't tell his Minister, or not just yet. He hadn't a pattern which fitted, and a couple of incidents, very probably connected but lacking a firm connection, wasn't something to offer a busy Minister. Mr Gabriel Palliser would already know about the evening fracas at the Imperial Circle—know and be unwelcomely involved. The morning papers had splashed the story, treating it according to their political complexions as an intolerable affront by a foreigner, a Slav at that, or as something which that old fool Merridew had been asking for for years. That was awkward, but the experienced Mr Palliser could live with it. Mutual apologies would already be flying between the Circle and Gorjan's embassy, but there would be more to the exchanges than polite apologies. If Gorjan was as ill as he seemed to be he might be in hospital for weeks, and that could be more than awkward. The Confederate Republic wouldn't like it; they'd be suspicious at best; they'd want him safely back, and quick. The ambassador would be telephoning, amongst others to Palliser. Who had enough of his plate already.

Russell smiled urbanely. The ambassador *had* been telephoning —to him, Charles Russell. They were very old friends.

He looked at his clock. His appointment with His Excellency was for a quarter-past ten and he had a quarter of an hour to wait still. He walked to a safe, unlocking it, taking out Gorjan's dossier. It wasn't the file he would have liked, the rounded picture he insisted on for any Englishman, but the facts were there and it was possible to clothe them. He began to read steadily.

A man, he thought, a genuine male animal. They weren't so common. Alexander Gorjan was a communist, but Russell mistrusted political labels. He'd have been a communist himself if he'd been of Gorjan's race. Come to think of it he'd helped them. He'd been dropped in the war into what was later to become the Confederate Republic and had spent three fruitful months there. He'd loathed the country but liked the people. Clearly Gorjan had their virtues. He was a scientist of world stature, so he must be outstandingly intelligent, and most of his compatriots were hardly that. But he hadn't allowed it to set him apart. He worked and he worked—God, how he seemed to work—but he also found time to live. Why not? A world-class scientist was a national asset, and the Confederate Republic put a very proper value on a national asset. Gorjan felt a need? Then society filled it. Not that his tastes were finicky—Russell approved them since he hadn't always been sixty. Doctor Gorjan liked slim fast cars; he liked wine and the best of food; and above all he liked women, lots of women. Charles Russell smiled again. This wasn't the picture of a scientist's traditional austerity. And all the time Gorjan worked. Between the meals, the excellent local Riesling, the troops and parades of strapping girls, he worked. Now he'd worked himself into the Hemmingway Hospital. Gorjan had had it coming but he wasn't the sort to complain or whine.

Russell put the file away. He must meet this Gorjan and meant to. Language wouldn't be a difficulty. If his remarks at the Circle had been correctly reported Gorjan must have a remarkable command of English.

The intercom purred discreetly and Russell pressed the switch.

'The ambassador to see you by appointment, sir.'

'Have him shown up, please.'

Nikola Mitrovic walked in. He walked firmly but lightly still, unmistakably a southern Slav. He had the peasant's solid figure and a large moustache. Russell noticed that it wasn't quite as big as once it had been—Excellencies must eschew extremes—but it was still a splendid growth. He was middle-aged now and maybe more, but he didn't invite a liberty. Russell had never intended one.

His Excellency said pleasantly: 'We don't see as much of each other as we used to.'

'That must be remedied.'

'They were good in their way, those days. The fighting——'

'I didn't do much fighting.'

'You do yourself less than justice. Your job was to give us arms, and of course to advise us. We took the arms, but I don't remember that we ever paid attention to the other. What I did have to do was to detail two men to watch you day and night. It would have been excessively awkward if a British liaison officer had been shot where he shouldn't have been.'

'I never liked your enemies.'

On an inflection of inquiry Mitrovic said: 'We can talk on that basis?'

'Frankly, I expected to.'

'Good. Then you'll have heard about Alexander Gorjan.'

'The affair at the Circle last night? I've read the papers.'

'Not only that. We sent him here, you know.'

'I know he could hardly have come here without your President's approval.'

'He had very much more than that. We *sent* him. You take what I'm trying to say?'

'I'm not sure I do.'

His Excellency played with his fine moustache. 'Then I'll have to explain, though I suspect you already know much of it. You know enough about my country to be certain that we're communists, but there are more sorts of Marxist than one. There are Leninists and Stalinites, or rather there were, there are Trotskyites, the Chinese, back-to-the-book boys, deviationists——'

'I'm not a theologian.'

'*Touché*.' Nikola Mitrovic laughed. 'Let's leave it that we're nationalists—we always were. That may be within the orthodox canon though more probably it isn't: the fact remains that a genuinely independent Confederate Republic has never really suited a much more powerful neighbour. The scales go up and down of course, there are comings and goings to Moscow, frowns one year, smiles the next. But basically it's a matter of power politics. None of us believes that if we weakened we could stand.'

'And nor do I.'

'I'm glad. But the word you have to listen to is "us". We, the old ones—the President, myself, the men you lay in ditches with. But you can never be sure about the younger generation. I was reminding you that there was more than one sort of communism, and one of our men in fifty, say, embraces a different kind. Mostly they're the younger ones. You were talking about theology and I'll gladly steal your metaphor.

17

The really religious man puts his creed above all else. Even before his country.' Mitrovic wasn't laughing now. 'Naturally he gets *used*. There's a conflict you see, and there always has been. I think there always will be. We're not cut out for satellite status.'

'I'd hate to try to rule you.'

'Quite. Making bad subjects is our major strength, but there's always been a neighbour anxious to, well, control us. So there's a struggle as I said, and it runs hot and cold. And sometimes it isn't what it seems to be—not from the West. Sometimes when the two of us are snarling we're snarling at nothing and know it, and sometimes when we're shaking hands we're really pretty desperate.' Mitrovic straightened suddenly. 'That happened last week and it was touch and go. Not a direct invasion—not if they could help it—but a snatch at power internally. It isn't impossible, it never is. Not even here. The army is sound enough but you know where we have to keep it. By the time it got back to the capital everything could be over, help asked for and given, the usual technique. It's happened before in other states and it's always been irreversible.' Mitrovic hesitated, then said firmly: 'We had to get Gorjan out.'

'He's really as big as that?'

'To us he is. You know what his line is—radar. And radar means interception.' The heavy shoulders rose and fell. 'Not that I believe he could get on to anything which Russian resources couldn't develop too, but he might get there first.'

'I see. And you think he has?'

'I'm not a scientist. I said I thought he might. And if I think so, so could our neighbours. . . .'

'Tricky,' Charles Russell said.

'For us, very tricky.' His Excellency rose, walking to the wall. Staring at a mezzotint, his broad back still to Russell, Mitrovic said softly: 'I've come to ask a favour.'

'Yes?'

'I said there was a crisis and there is. Normally they last a week and then we know where we are. We've cards, you see, and plenty of practice at playing them. The Old Man's very skilful. Yes, we normally know in a week or so; we breathe again.' Mitrovic swung suddenly. 'But not this time,' he said.

'The pot's still boiling? I didn't know that.'

'Why should you? Reading the English papers you'd think we were on a honeymoon with our dear friends further east. We keep these matters quiet, you know, and your embassy in my country. . . .' Mitrovic smiled politely.

'Yes, I know about our embassies; I see their stuff. Our ambassadors' despatches waste my time.' Russell waved at the empty chair and Mitrovic sat down again. 'And this favour you were asking me?'

'Keep Gorjan here a bit. Of course we could simply tell him to stay, but it would look decidedly suspicious having a perfectly healthy Gorjan hanging about in England doing nothing. Your papers would smell a rat at once and I told you we like to keep our troubles to ourselves.'

Russell asked blandly: 'You mean we should find a job for him?'

'You know he wouldn't work for you. We couldn't permit it and he wouldn't want to. I just want him *kept* here.'

'Then how do you suggest?'

'I don't presume to.'

Charles Russell shook his head. 'It isn't on. I haven't a motive, either—rather to the contrary. Why should we hold your hot potato? In any case I don't think it's really necessary. Gorjan seems pretty ill. You're a fine healthy man yourself and I doubt if you know much about psychiatrists. The reputation of the Hemmingway Hospital is that it's easy enough to get into but a whole lot harder to get out. I don't think it's likely that they'll bundle Gorjan on to an aircraft for your country simply because he's recovered enough to stand the journey.'

'You find him a hot potato, then?'

'I do.' Russell had taken an immediate decision; he wouldn't play ball with a half-baked idea, but he'd pass information. Mitrovic, indeed, had a right to this special piece of it. Russell said evenly, watching Mitrovic: 'Did you know there was an attempt on Gorjan's life last night?'

The ambassador sat motionless. His eyes had narrowed in an expression Russell recognized. He looked solider than ever—dangerous. This wasn't an Excellency but again a fighting man. He began to bark briefly: 'You've got the men?'

'We have.'

'How many men, please?'

'Two.'

'Nationality?'

'Yours. There's a near-colony of your people here and on the face of it they're runaways from your own brand of communism. But we've known for some time that several were more than that. Naturally we've been watching them, but so far they hadn't bothered us. These two, as it happened, were new arrivals, so what we want now is their contacts.'

'They've talked yet?' Mitrovic asked.

'Not yet.'

'They'll talk in time?'

'In time. Remember this is England.'

Nikola Mitrovic went silent. He had been a first-class commander of irregular troops but he preferred to see his enemy in front of him. Thought in the abstract, a nice decision between conflicting courses, had never come easily. He liked to think slowly and he was confident Russell would let him. This was more serious than he had known. He had known that he had enemies in London but not that they were organized. Gorjan had collapsed and had been taken to the Hemmingway. Which couldn't have been foreseen. Yet within hours they had moved against him. So either an unexpected opportunity had been acted on very quickly, or else an existing plan had been switched with a frightening competence. It was sobering even to hear of, though good might come out of it yet. For Russell had taken the men concerned; no doubt they were being held in one of the discreet hideaways which the Executive would be maintaining. They'd talk in time, even in England they always broke in time, and they'd implicate those who worked with them. Then Russell would act. It was no part of his duty to support the Republic against its enemies, but it was very much his business to prevent those enemies mounting a murder in England. The political complications could be incalculable, and the English detested the incalculable. Mitrovic knew his Russell.

He looked up at him quickly but his face told him nothing. Mitrovic sighed softly. Russell would deal with the refugees. Disaffected men or dangerous he'd find English ways to block them; he'd deal with the body, but the brains, the ambassador thought, what seemed to be the leader. . . .

He would have given a great deal to be able to tell Russell about Stevan Starc. Starc was his own First Secretary, but Mitrovic had just received a tip-off. It hadn't astonished him that there was an agent in his embassy. There was already a safe which he couldn't open without the help of quite a junior member of his staff, and he was perfectly aware that his personal servant held the rank of major in an organization which certainly wasn't the diplomatic corps. What had astonished him —frightened him too—was to discover that the agent wasn't his own. There had been an immediate exchange of telegrams in a code used only in emergencies, and very much the answer which Mitrovic had expected. Starc had been screened from birth and there was nothing against him. But His Excellency's telegram hadn't been pooh-poohed. Starc's record was impeccable but he could always have defected.

In eastern Europe defector was the worst word known. Defection to the West was bad, but one which looked eastwards to the final enemy a great deal worse. Stevan Starc was a traitor.

Another telegram had followed and with it decision. This was too serious to be solved by a recall. A simple recall might simply be disobeyed, and if Starc went underground in London an important lead would go with him. His Excellency would know the situation at home, and leads of this sort could be immensely valuable domestically. A specialist would be despatched as soon as he could be relieved of his present assignment. Rank in embassy to be Third Secretary. The other didn't matter. But he'd have to be briefed and accredited and it would all take some time. Meanwhile there was Petar.

Nikola Mitrovic sighed again. Petar was his servant and an experienced man, but he wasn't a young one. In Mitrovic's service London was considered a quiet-ish post and quiet-ish men were sent there. Petar was one of them. He was clever at his job, which was collecting information and sending it—microfilms and microdots, all the apparatus of the earnest spy. But what was now needed was some tough young operator, somebody who could shadow Starc, a resourceful man, ruthless if required, and. . . .

And Russell would have a dozen such. His Excellency would have given his pension to be able to tell Charles Russell about Starc. Russell could tide him over till this specialist in defectors could arrive.

Unconsciously he shook his head. He couldn't use Russell, then ask him to lay off again. One time he might have but not, it seemed, now. Mitrovic didn't blame him: twenty years had rolled over both of them.

So he'd have to rely on Petar and it mightn't be enough.

He rose a little heavily and left.

CHAPTER 3

Stevan Starc lived in a service flat at the southern end of Luxborough Street, looking across Paddington Street to the gardens which had once been a cemetery. It was a modest flat, and in it he did such entertaining as was required of him. That too was modest, for the Confederate Republic was too realistic to suppose that lavishly entertaining other diplomats was the way to advance a country's interests, and the serious entertaining of serious Englishmen was done by the ambassador himself. The area was central, and there were a good many other foreigners, though not of his own kind. That suited Starc. He had been using the Bear and Staff for several months and by now he was accepted there.

And something more, since the barmaid was his carrier. She took messages and delivered them, messages to those who shared a common ideology. Starc had assessed her carefully. She came from south London and he had decided at once that the least smell of politics, international politics in particular, would scare her into uselessness. So he had pretended to be a thief.

He had flashed a fat roll, watching her small eyes glitter with a sudden sharp cupidity; he had dropped phrases of thieves' and con men's slang; he had given her a wrist watch which, though valuable, was evidently not quite new; and he had always been very generous in payment. His first two messages she had steamed open at home. Starc had expected it and they had been nonsense about some non-existent job. He had estimated her correctly. Politics were dangerous and even the possibility of treason terrifying. But nowadays stealing hardly counted, did it? Besides it was exciting, a change from the telly at home. Now she was his drop.

Starc was walking to the Bear and Staff after the worst day he could remember. There had been nothing from his two best men and he realized what that meant. Moreover, the failure was wholly his, since it had been his own decision to send them to the Hemmingway. There hadn't been time for consultation. He had heard the attendant of the ambulance talking about the Hemmingway Hospital and it had seemed an opportunity which they couldn't afford to miss. They had always assumed that Gorjan would be guarded and would stay so throughout his visit. Their original plan had allowed for that, but like all plans to kill a guarded man it wouldn't have been infallible. Now their carefully considered plan had gone, but that could cut both ways. This might be opportunity, wide open. A sudden change of schedule to a hospital in a suburb. . . .

Starc had risked a telephone, telling his men that the existing plan was cancelled. They were to follow to the Hemmingway and take their chance there. Now he was wishing he hadn't. Failure wasn't something his masters accepted easily, and the only two men he thought of as proper agents hadn't reported. Starc indeed knew what that meant. They might hold for a while but not for ever, for he was under no illusion that in the matter of interrogation British security would pay too much attention to the Judges' Rules. Sooner or later they'd admit his connection with them but he'd face that when he came to it. Meanwhile the small fry knew him only as a number which sent them orders, but the lower they lay the better. He owed them a warning and he owed himself time to think. So he was walking to the Bear and Staff with the message to his contacts of every agent under pressure. Disperse. If caught keep your mouth shut.

He went the way he always did, walking across Paddington Street and turning into Ashland Place. Ashland, he supposed, was some English landlord's name but 'Place' was pretentious. The lane was eight feet wide at most. The wall of the old cemetery was on Starc's right, three feet of brickwork topped by chain fencing, and, on his left, the almost unbroken backs of what he had learnt were Buildings. They were working-class flats. Their doors were in another street but the windows of the living rooms, low against the pavement, looking into Ashland Place. They were heavily curtained and Starc had always thought them very cosy. There were warm lights behind them and the chatter of television. Stevan Starc smiled. Behind him was the comparative bustle of Paddington Street, away to his right, beyond the cemetery, a modern office block. Here he was in another world, almost another century.

He had been thinking about his errand, and for the first time he noticed that he was walking in the dark. Normally the little lane was lighted by four lamps spaced one at each end and two in the middle, riding high on the Buildings' wall, electric now but elegant old things still. Tonight they weren't working. There was the faintest glow from behind the snug curtained windows; a stripling moon chased cumulus across the sky. And that was all—that and the old cemetery. One or two graves had been left. Starc would have admitted that it was a little eerie.

He felt in his pocket for a torch, stopping to do so, and twenty yards behind him a man stopped too.

Starc froze against the wall. He knew at once that someone was shadowing him and he weighed the chances coolly. It might be a cosh man and that would be lucky. Starc wasn't afraid of cosh men. Or again it might not and that wouldn't be lucky at all. He considered the window behind him but dismissed it. It was too solid to crash, and if he knocked they would be frightened. Even if they opened there would be explanations, talk, and Stevan Starc detested explanations. He looked at the wire on the cemetery wall. He could make it perhaps but it wasn't a working risk. Caught half-way over, a man would be quite defenceless. He looked down Ashland Place to Moxon Street. He could run for it—so could the other. Besides if he ran he'd never know. Cosh man or something else. . . .

The difference was important.

Deliberately Starc walked back to the other man. He didn't move. Starc wasn't armed but that didn't worry him. He had switched off his torch but now he turned it on again. He flashed it in the other's face.

Quite suddenly he was furious. Petar! They'd put Petar on his tail. Petar was fifty, an old, old man, a snapper-up of trifles from impoverished government clerks. Petar was a petty spy: this was an insult. Petar!

Without speaking Starc seized his shoulders. He shook him like a doormat, silent and savage. Petar twisted in his grip, but helplessly. Starc threw him against the wall and his head smashed against it. Petar staggered but did not fall.

Methodically Starc began to beat him. He hit him once in the face and twice in the stomach. Petar groaned softly and began to fold. Starc took his collar, pulling him upright. He raised his free hand and the knife came up to him. It was shatteringly unexpected and a bare inch off target. Starc felt blood on his cheek but below the eye. He caught the knife and put it in his pocket. Petar didn't resist him now. Starc smashed him down again, then, with a quiet brutality, kicked him insensible. Petar didn't utter.

When it was done Starc searched him quickly, looking each way up Ashland Place, ready to run. He took Petar's wallet, his watch and a thin gold pencil. Then he straightened again, pulling up his scarf above his nose. There was fog and it wouldn't look unusual. There was blood inside his collar now and there seemed to be a lot of it. He couldn't patch this one up himself, he'd have to get attention. He slipped back to Paddington Street, looking both ways, and in the High Street he found a taxi. He gave it an address in Gilston Road. A Doctor Palfrey lived there though she didn't now practice. Margaret Palfrey called herself a literary journalist and broadcaster.

A procession of lovers had found a shorter word. Starc had been one of them. If, he thought grimly, 'lover' wasn't an indecency. Only the tightest discipline had kept him within a mile of her.

In the taxi he sat rigid. The blood had come down to his chest now, tickling him surprisingly, warm and disgusting. For a second he took his scarf off, looking at his reflection in the mirror inside the taxi. It was worse than he'd thought; it would be five or six stitches at least. He put up the scarf again, reversing it to hide the blood.

He paid the taxi quickly, and used the key she'd once given him to enter the flat. Margaret Palfrey was writing in the living-room. He'd always hated it. There were African woodcarvings on the mantelpiece, *avant garde* paintings and elaborate flowers which could have done with changing. This was Margaret Palfrey's room and it became her. Starc took off his scarf and waited.

· She ran to him with a little cry. 'Why Stevan. . . .'

He could have killed her with greater pleasure than he had beaten Petar. He'd known she'd give a little cry, he'd known she'd say: 'Why Stevan.' And now she went on stupidly: 'What's happened?'

He didn't answer. 'Do you remember enough to stitch me up?'

'I—I really don't know. I've a box still, I think, but it's fifteen years. I——'

'I'd be glad if you'd try.'

'There's a man round the corner.'

'I can't go to him.'

'But——'

He said fiercely: 'For Christ's sake stop talking. Work.'

She rose, but uncertainly, and he watched her fuss with water and a towel. She was astonishingly clumsy with her hands. Perhaps that was why she had never really practised. He watched her fumbling, over-pouring the disinfectant, almost upsetting the bowl. She was going to hurt him badly but he was good at pain. She swabbed off the blood and threaded a surgical needle.

'I'm afraid this is going to hurt.'

'Of course it is. Get it over.'

She sewed him up roughly, apologizing ceaselessly. He needed her, her almost forgotten skill. He thought of his need and not his loathing. . . . Having to go to bed with her, the avid shameless thing, the far Left conversation first, the baby-talk after. Not that she was quite ugly yet, simply horrible and degrading.

And a duty he'd been assigned to, one almost of routine. For Margaret was of the high rich Left, the world of Sir William Merridew, of strident progressive thinkers. Starc held it in a grim contempt, but it was something which no communist neglected, a richly stinking compost of petty treason. What swine they all were! Talking progressive politics on comfortable incomes, cutting competitive figures in a cardboard world. They'd never face reality—they needn't. They'd talk and they'd fellow-travel but they'd never know the passion. How indeed could they? Two hundred pounds a month of easy money. Often more. Of course they could never be taught or trained; no serious communist considered trying. But he'd recognize their usefulness. They'd do most things for a paragraph and treason for a headline. Christ, what a sewer.

Starc stared at Margaret Palfrey, hating her. She was looking for the scissors and it took her a minute to find them.

'I ought to put a bandage on.'

'No. Give me some plaster.'

She found it at last and the fumbling began again. He took it from her, cutting it neatly. The adhesive was almost gone, but he warmed it by the fire. With the first hint of firmness Margaret Palfrey said: 'And now we'll have a drink.'

'No thank you.'

He saw he had astonished her. She'd been expecting his story and a cosy chat, even, he thought disgustedly, a little of what passed for love. He picked up his hat and overcoat; the scarf he held out to her.

'Burn that.'

'But Stevan——'

'Burn it. And tell nobody I've been here, far less what for.' He faced her implacably. 'I'm quite sure you'll keep your mouth shut. I know who pays the rent, you see, and I know you don't want to lose him.'

He watched her face disintegrate, but quite without pity. It had been one of the things he'd despised in her most—that she lived on a rich American. She'd laughed at him and often sneered but she'd taken his money. Mellion Lee was sick with wealth and it came from his father's newspapers. He was a diplomat in London too, a Counsellor. Stevan Starc would have smiled if his wound had let him. That at least had been compensation: secretly cuckolding an American dear colleague hadn't been distasteful. He wondered what rich Americans did when the woman they were keeping was unfaithful. He knew what he'd do himself: he'd beat her a bit and leave her. But Americans, degenerates, might simply do nothing. The reflection was interesting but it wasn't important. For Mellion Lee would never know. They'd been very discreet indeed.

She began to cry but it didn't move him. Why, she couldn't even cry right. A woman should weep properly, decently discharging a decent grief. Margaret merely snivelled. He walked to the door and slammed it. Once in the street he spat.

He knew what he must do. Somebody had blown him—not the two men who hadn't reported, there hadn't been time to break them and British security wouldn't have been using Petar. But somebody had tipped off Mitrovic. It didn't matter who. A blown agent was useless—worse he was a danger. He must get underground and quick. . . . Just a man on the run, a creature without a future. Some time if he were lucky they would pull him out of England. Or more likely they wouldn't. He'd failed after all and that was fatal. There was a well-established method with those who failed.

Stevan Starc shrugged. He knew the rules and he wasn't a coward.

He found another taxi, giving it this time an address in north London. It wasn't his hideout, long prepared, but only within a mile of it. In the wilderness north of Highbury that was a very long way.

He sat motionless in the taxi. His future was unknown or worse but Starc was content. Margaret Palfrey was behind him. He fingered his plastered face. By God, she'd made a mess of it, but at least she'd patched him up enough not to attract attention. He'd allow her that single credit since they'd never meet again.

In that he was mistaken.

CHAPTER 4

There were standing orders to show Charles Russell any police report concerning diplomats or those who directly served them, and there was one on top of his pile next morning. The personal servant of the ambassador of the Confederate Republic had been assaulted and robbed in Marylebone; he'd been handled very heavily and he wasn't as young as he had been. With luck he'd recover consciousness, but it wasn't certain that he could identify his assailant. The lights in Ashland Place had failed, and in any case there might have been a mask. The lane had been a set-up for a coshing. Russell walked to the map of London on the wall; he found Ashland Place but only by looking hard; then, back at his desk, he asked for a number.

The Security Executive didn't tail diplomats, even Iron Curtain diplomats, or not as a matter of course. Several it must, and these it accepted as both normal duties and legitimate risks. Petar hadn't been one of them. Russell knew he was a spy but he considered him small beer. Moreover he'd cracked his network. From time to time he fed titbits into it, checking on their disposal. So nobody had been on Petar's tail, but Petar didn't live in Marylebone or anywhere near it. Therefore he had probably had a contact there and Russell didn't know of one. The implication was that there might have been a slip-up, so Russell had just telephoned to what the Executive called an area representative. They were field men in fact, and the local police, when sufficiently senior, were trusted with their identities but not much more. They were seldom put on specific jobs—in their way they were much too valuable to risk— but their knowledge of their territories was absolute. In the postal district of London West One Russell had three of them. When the call came through he said: 'Secure?'

'Secure, sir.'

'Then there's been a report about a man called Petar. He didn't live in your manor but he was coshed and robbed in it. He was nominally the manservant of the ambassador of the Confederate Republic but he was also a minor spy. We know most things about him but not why he went to Marylebone. Had he anything there?'

'A contact, you mean? If he had it was a very new.' The voice was confident.

'Any national of the Confederacy living in the area? Ex-national?'

'Only one. It isn't their stamping ground. They cluster in Canonbury, or the richer round Camden Hill.'

'And what about the one?'

'He's a diplomat called Starc, First Secretary at their embassy. He lives in Luxborough Street, the other end from Madame Tussaud's.'

'But that's right on top of Ashland Place. Where Petar was coshed.'

'I doubt if your man was visiting Starc, sir. Socially they're in different worlds. Petar, you say, was a servant, and Stevan Starc was a First Secretary.' There was a dry little chuckle. 'No one is quite so protocol-conscious as a communist embassy. And meeting for business would have been absurdly insecure. Unnecessary too—they could have seen each other daily at their jobs. I know one thing about Starc which interests me, and that I'm not sure of or I'd have sent it in already. He uses the Bear and Staff a lot, and I've sometimes wondered about the barmaid. She has very expensive jewellery and she's just bought a Minicar. She could be a spy of sorts, most probably just a carrier, though there are earthier explanations of a barmaid's sudden wealth. I'm morally certain she wasn't carrying for Petar, and if Starc has been using her for purposes of his own, then Petar still doesn't fit in. Why should Starc drop a message in the Bear and Staff for Petar? They could meet at the embassy.'

'I agree I wouldn't have reported that—not as it stands. But Ashland Place is remarkably close to Luxborough Street and I never feel quite happy with coincidence.' Russell's voice changed decisively. 'Sniff around it a bit and report again quickly.'

He lit the first pipe of the day, thinking of Nikola Mitrovic. Russell had known more about the situation in the Confederate Republic than he had admitted to him. Despatches from Her Majesty's ambassadors were notoriously misleading, but the Security Executive wasn't confined to official sources for its assessments of foreign countries. So Russell had at once accepted what Mitrovic had told him. A snatch at power internally—Nikola had used the phrase and Russell hadn't discounted it. There was a crisis in the Confederacy, one which a neighbour would certainly exploit if indeed they hadn't started it. The founding fathers were getting old, the President was seventy. And those who would come after them, those who stood next in line? There were more sorts of communists than one: that had been another of Nikola's little *mots*. There were the old ones—communists certainly but patriots first. Bloody bourgeois nationalists, or some might think so. Nikola had said some did, some of the younger ones. Who'd be naturals as earnest dupes for their country's ancestral enemy.

Charles Russell sighed. He had said he wasn't a theologian, but you needed at least a taste for theology to thread the maze of communist doctrine. Dominicans, he remembered, said that Jesuits were Pelagians, which had been a very dangerous label in the forum of the faithful. And communists had words like deviationist. That was at least as dangerous, at least as likely to see you at the stake. It depended who held the matches.

Russell began on routine work, conscious that he was waiting on his telephone. Half an hour later it rang. A voice said cautiously: 'West London One, north end. I think I'm going to surprise you, sir.'

'I try never to be surprised.'

28

'*I* was. I've done my sniffing and there's quite a smell.' There was a well-timed pause. 'Starc seems to have disappeared.'

'You mean he's gone?' Russell's voice hadn't altered.

'Gone with the wind.'

'Does anybody know it yet?'

'Only the porter at his block of flats. I'll come to the porter later, sir. Otherwise nobody knows yet.'

'And how, if I may ask, do you?'

'I've had a look at his flat. There's a service door to the block and that was easy. So was his own lock. There was nobody about.'

'And what did you find?'

'Bed hadn't been slept in and nothing had been disturbed. Wardrobe seemed full. No signs of packing. That was negative, of course.'

'It was. So what did you do?'

'I got myself out again and rang the porter. Starc might have left a number. When it was clear he hadn't I didn't actually say that I was ringing from his embassy, but I put on a foreign accent. I said I couldn't contact Monsieur Starc; I hinted he hadn't been quite as well as usual and I tried to sound worried. The porter asked me to hang on. I don't know what happened but I assume he went upstairs and used his pass key. When he came back *he* sounded worried. He had a woman with him, the housekeeper I expect, and I overheard them talking about Starc's habits. He'd never gone away before without giving notice. Then the porter started on me again; he began to ask questions, but I thanked him and rang off. I imagine he'll give it an hour or two, then go to the police to cover himself.'

'Saving us trouble.'

'You don't want me to follow up?'

'Not yet. Missing persons are police work, or at any rate to start with. And the Press will be on to this too. Diplomat Disappears from Luxury Flat.' Russell was talking in headlines. 'Why is it always a *luxury* flat? I'd rather the police dealt with that side. He's a diplomat too—that's tricky. So just for the moment lay off. And thank you. You've done very well.'

Charles Russell sat back. . . . So an ambassador's servant had been coshed and robbed, or that was what it looked like, since stealing a man's valuables wasn't conclusive that the real motive for the crime was robbery. And quite a senior official of the same embassy, one living near the scene of the assault, had incontinently bolted. Behind all this a very distinguished scientist from the country in question had been deliberately sent to England and within hours of his arrival had almost been murdered by men whose nationality was known. Which was the same as Petar's, the same as Starc's, the same, for that matter, as Gorjan's himself. But Gorjan's breakdown at the Imperial Circle had been unforeseen and so had his removal to the Hemmingway. Starc, on the other hand, had been present at the Circle, and the crew of the ambulance hadn't concealed its destination. Therefore Starc could have passed it to the two would-be killers, indeed if he hadn't it was guesswork who had. Russell wouldn't know for certain till the two men started talking, but that could take some time. He had given instructions for their interrogation but had limited them scrupulously. He was head of security but he wasn't a barbarian. Even so the pieces fitted and the pattern they made was alarming. The sooner a Minister knew about this the happier Russell would be.

For a moment he hesitated. He had facts which fitted neatly but he hadn't a shred of proof. Not that its lack was fatal. Mr Gabriel Palliser wasn't a civil servant. On the contrary his mistrust of them was notorious and reciprocated.

Nevertheless the habits of bureaucracy weren't all contemptible and Russell used such as served him. He began to write deliberately:

1. There is a crisis in the Confederate Republic, partly internal, young men against old ones, but with a much more powerful neighbour backing the young. Mitrovic didn't try to hide it.

2. Alexander Gorjan, a pre-eminent scientist and a national asset, is despatched abroad to keep him out of danger.

3. There is then an attempt to kill him by two young compatriots illegally in England. There is a prima facie connection between them and Stevan Starc, though we are unlikely to establish it firmly for some time if ever. Starc is First Secretary in Mitrovic's embassy, and Nikola is clearly a worried man.

4. Mitrovic's servant is beaten up within a stone's throw of Starc's flat. Any connection with Starc is entirely putative, since the servant is unconscious still and in any case may not recognize his assailant (or may not wish to). But Petar is other things besides his ambassador's servant and it is perfectly possible that he knew too much about Starc for comfort.

5. Starc disappears the same night.

6. One assumption holds these incidents together. It is an assumption, but against the background of what is happening in the Republic it is tenable or better. It is that Starc has been double-crossing Mitrovic. That implies that he is working for exactly the Power whose activities made it necessary to send Gorjan to England.

Russell read this carefully and nodded. It wasn't a story to tell a judge but it was one to tell Gabriel Palliser. He telephoned to his office. Mr Palliser had gone down to his constituency but he would be back tomorrow. Very well then, Colonel Russell would be sending him a report first thing in the morning. It would arrive by safe-hand messenger who would want the Minister's own signature for its delivery. Russell himself would be arriving for discussion half an hour behind this messenger. Say at ten o'clock. . . . But half-past ten would be more convenient? Then it was half-past ten precisely.

Alexander Gorjan had woken from an afternoon asleep. He knew at once that he was very much better. He wasn't in pain, his eye was clear, and whatever drug they had been giving him had worked itself out of his system. This had happened before and he knew the symptoms. He was well again till next time. He sat up in bed and called the nurse.

'Give me a drink, please.'

'I'll get you some tea.'

'To hell with tea. I want some wine.'

The black nurse hesitated. An important gentleman, an ambassador they'd told her, had called the day before. Gorjan had been sleeping and they hadn't thought wise to wake him, but the important-looking gentleman had certainly brought wine—wine and cigars and an armful of books and newspapers in a language she couldn't read. There hadn't been space for all of it in matron's room so they'd put it in the cupboard in her patient's. Who was now saying firmly: 'I know there'll be wine. My friends will have sent it.'

The nurse was in a difficulty. She hadn't authority to give Gorjan wine, indeed she suspected it would be most irregular. On the other hand she couldn't afford a scene with him. Matron would be just as severe with her if a patient became excited as she would if he drank a glass of wine. Which in any case she might never hear about, or not till after drink had been allowed. Matron's prim lips would purse, matron would look disapproving. Matron was very good at that and the black nurse resented it.

She went to the cupboard and opened a bottle. There was a label in the language she couldn't read, but it was wine all right. It was a straw-coloured thing, alive, and it smelt delicious. She brought a glass of it to the bed but Gorjan didn't take it.

'I can't drink alone.'

The nurse hesitated again. One thing she was certain of: she oughtn't to drink with patients, especially those who smiled at her. She was thinking he was a very good-looking man. He had a deep flat chest and a lock of hair, shot faintly with a badger's grey, fell carelessly across an eye. The eye was blue and the voice was deep. The nurse said in a small one: 'I——'

He smiled again and she caught her breath. 'Come on—we're quite alone.'

31

They were, she thought, at that. She poured another glass and brought it.

'That's better. Sit down. No, not on that chair. The bed.'

'Oh no.'

He showed white teeth again. 'Don't be so haughty. It's a very good bed. How long have I been in it?'

'Two nights and a day. And what's gone of this one.'

'It often takes longer when I've had one of these spasms. You've looked after me very well. You've earned your wine and somewhere comfortable to drink it.' He patted the blanket. 'Come on.'

The nurse giggled but sat down.

He pinched her bottom reflectively. He was thinking again how handsome she was. A fine full figure and a tiny waist. She was black as a sentry's boot but damned attractive. She knew it too—enjoyed it. She'd squeaked discreetly when he'd pinched her bottom but it hadn't been louder than was expected of a lady. He could see she was that, and he used the word precisely. She hadn't slapped his face. Not that that would have meant a thing.

He drank his wine, not asking for more. One had to be sensible with the first drink for days, and sensible about the black nurse too. Later, no doubt—he could see it was mutual. He'd never possessed a black one yet and that was a gap to fill.

Colonel Charles Russell was walking back to the Executive from his interview with his Minister. Mr Gabriel Palliser wasn't popular in Whitehall, but Russell admired him. He wasn't popular with senior civil servants because he treated them with less than the deference which, after a generation of broken-backed Ministers, they considered they were entitled to, and he wasn't much loved by fellow Ministers for the rather different reason that he made his mind up quickly and could be relied on not to change it. That was awkward for weaker brethren: it was even an embarrassment to a Cabinet which would do anything but commit itself and stand. But for the head of the Security Executive Gabriel Palliser had the essential virtues, which in order of importance to him were loyalty and decision. Privately Russell considered him a little flash: he dressed a thought too carefully, he took a little too long with a gold cigarette case. And at heart he was a cynic. Russell knew him socially and once they had dined alone. Palliser, after a drink or two, had ventured a quotation: 'Men are wicked, and when I die I shall at least have the consolation of never having rendered one a service.' Russell had thought it an over-statement but he hadn't been shocked. Mr Gabriel Palliser was an excellent Minister and that was what counted. He knew his own job and respected you when you did. He didn't, for instance, ask questions he shouldn't; he hadn't distressed himself that the Security Executive was holding two foreigners in circumstances which would have outraged a court. Mr Palliser wasn't a lawyer.

But he had read Russell's report and had grasped its implications instantly; he had been reasonable and even helpful. . . . So there were refugees from the Confederate Republic who weren't what they seemed to be; they were in fact working for another Power, traitors to their own country, and two of them had tried to kill its most important citizen. Mr Palliser wouldn't speak of those two but the rest must be mopped up promptly, since any risk of a second attempt on Gorjan was obviously unacceptable. But Russell would have a line on the small fry quite apart from the men he held. This barmaid was probably only a carrier but, suitably frightened, she would be able to identify photographs. No doubt Russell had them. Then a deportation or two, discreet ones, real reasons suppressed. He'd fix it with the Home Office, which was co-operative enough provided you kept the lawyers out.

That would bag the low numbers.

Which left Stevan Starc, who was rather more delicate. Russell's report had been on Palliser's desk and the Minister had nodded at it. The assumption was that Starc was at the bottom of all this, the brains behind these tiresome refugees. That wasn't yet certain but Palliser would accept it since there wasn't a better hypothesis. Then somehow his own embassy had rumbled him and had put on a man to watch him. Who hadn't been very good at it. Starc had beaten him up and vanished. That was police work if it was anybody's: Russell had done wisely to keep out of it. But to implicate Starc in attempted murder Russell would be dependent on a certain two men talking. No doubt they would have valuable information about other matters too, and Palliser didn't intend to make security more difficult than he knew it already was. So let them talk and the more the better. But if they implicated Starc in an attempt to murder Gorjan, that, it seemed clear, was a write-off. For one thing the evidence could never be used, and for another. . . .

The Minister had cocked a firm black eyebrow. But how much did Starc matter now? He was formally still a diplomat, which was a dangerously explosive property often better left alone. And it was unlikely that he would be active again, or not for a while. Duly accredited diplomats couldn't expect to disappear without attracting attention, so Starc would know that the police at least would be something more than interested in his whereabouts. Also he would presumably read the papers still. He'd have to lie low—assuming, that is, that he hadn't already been spirited out of the country. Which seemed quite a big assumption. In any case Russell would be on notice now and notice was half the battle. There was a couple of hoodlums still being questioned, but Russell wouldn't be holding them if he hadn't also plans for their disposal. Impetuous action was always fatal and Russell was too experienced to have risked it. Of course if Starc had a hideout and these bastards put Russell on to it, that might be awkward, but Palliser's own belief was that the bird had already flown. Frankly, his hope too. Russell could report again and they'd cross that bridge when they came to it.

Russell had nodded, rising to leave, but Palliser waved him down again. He offered his extravagant gold cigarette case and when they were alight said quietly: 'It looks fairly tidy, doesn't it? But I remember you once told me that nothing so much scared you as a case which looked open and shut.'

Charles Russell sat up sharply. 'I believe you've a hunch. Ministers with hunches are something I listen to.'

'Not a hunch. I've been doing some thinking, that's all. Political thinking. It's what I'm allegedly paid for.' Mr Palliser rubbed his chin. 'It's a very unusual set-up, quite a change from the orthodox fuss about some secret. Gorjan hasn't got one—we all seem agreed on that. What he does have is an outstanding position in the world of radar, and radar today means early warning first. And missile-interference afterwards. A real breakthrough in either would be worth a thousand rockets. We're none of us saying Gorjan has got it but we're all of us accepting that his reputation justifies the fear he might.'

'I notice you said "the fear". Who's fearing?'

'You're remarkably quick, so ask yourself this. Which side would press the buttons first? There's something they call first strike, I think. Whose strategy *dictates* first strike? And who would most suffer if it wasn't as effective as the button-pushers had gambled on?'

There was a considerable silence; finally Russell said: 'So the attempt to kill Gorjan was an attempt to *deny*. Denial to the enemy—that was the army phrase for it.'

'There was another convenient cliché—exploitation.'

'Ye-es. Which the side with the overwhelming counter-strike but strategically on the defensive would just as logically be interested in—to *use* Gorjan instead of killing him. I agree with that as argument, but do you think in practice they'd go after it?'

'I think they've already started. Have you heard of a man called Mellion Lee?'

'I've met a Mellion Lee at the American Embassy. He was Counsellor (Scientific).' The brackets were ironically made audible. 'A tall man in English clothes but with all the right Washington connections.'

'You don't sound as though you liked him.'

'I like Americans but I like them American. This one's been here too long.'

Palliser said thoughtfully: 'I'm not sure you're wholly right. He may fancy our tailors but he hasn't gone Anglophile. You know these New England brahmins. They're deceptively British till there's a straight clash of interests, then they'll put you against the wall without apology. So I've met Lee socially more often than you, and he rang me last night.' Palliser smiled wryly. 'Officially it was a private call but in practice it certainly wasn't. Lee was talking about Gorjan, and in effect he congratulated us on Gorjan's breakdown. He'd be here for some time by all accounts, and perhaps we had ideas for using it. Then Lee talked about other things a bit, things where they hold the screw on us. He did it very well indeed—nothing he'd mind a tape of if I'd happened to be taking one. I wasn't. But he made himself perfectly clear. They wanted their piece of anything Gorjan gave us. They wanted it or else.'

'But what could Gorjan give us?'

'Nothing. Naturally I'd thought of it—in principle, I mean. But it simply isn't on. The man's a communist, a patriot too. He may not love the Russians and I suspect he loathes their guts, but that doesn't mean he'd work for us. We're decadent West like the others. What could we do in any case? He isn't a man to bribe and I'm sure he wouldn't frighten. And the least hint that we were squeezing him and they'd move him elsewhere tomorrow.'

'Lee must know that.'

'I dare say he does. What he rang me for was to stake their claim on anything we might happen to stumble on. In our lackadaisical English way. But that doesn't exclude that they'll also act directly. This Lee's on the List as Counsellor (Scientific). What would you think that means?'

'Probably more than usual. He's a Counsellor by right and rank and we know he's had some sort of scientific background. The usual form is to hire some fourth-rate scientist and tag him as a diplomat. Lee's more effective than that.'

The Minister frowned. 'Effective enough to start something?'

'The word I don't like is "start". They could make an appalling mess of it. They could land us all in international queer street.'

'Russell, you read my thoughts. You're a pleasure to do business with.'

'But I'm not very sure I can help you.'

'I just thought you should know of it. You can tell me things when you fancy it and when you don't you needn't.' The Minister smiled again, not wryly now. 'I know you don't always bother me and I'm telling you I accept it.'

Charles Russell had gone back to the Security Executive but not at once to work. . . . What a card to come up in a nice quiet game! Killing he knew about and secrets too. Secrets meant spying, squalid more often than conventionally exciting, chases across the bad lands after what were called the papers. But this wasn't a secret, it was Gorjan's *mind*. That went with a body, so those who wished to destroy the mind need only destroy the man. That was simple—old hat. But those who planned to exploit the mind must first control the body.

Russell sat down at his desk again. He'd been thinking in his accustomed terms, of a counter-operation against an all too familiar enemy. Now he didn't have an enemy, only his country's allies and they scared him. They'd go after Gorjan. They wouldn't try to kill him since a radar man dead was unexploitable. But they'd go for his mind.

. . . Making a shocking mess of it, landing us all in international queer street.

There was a transatlantic Agency of matchless resources and competence. Russell respected it, playing ball happily with its London representative. But this wasn't the Agency but a politically-connected diplomat. This was going to be the amateurs, something the Executive called Embassy Intelligence.

In the world of professionals that was feared worse than death.

Charles Russell shrugged. He had a plateful again and he didn't like the look of it.

CHAPTER 5

Half a lifetime of unobtrusive service to his country's interests had taught Charles Russell patience. Though Gabriel Palliser's reminder against impetuous action had been delicately delivered it had also been unnecessary, since going off at half-cock wasn't one of Russell's failings. He knew that he must now await developments, but that was something he was used to and accepted. He had accepted, too, that what he would now be faced with was precisely what scared him most: Embassy Intelligence, the amateurs. It wasn't a situation which any professional would look forward to with confidence—amateurs were incalculable—but at least he could foresee a move ahead even if he could do nothing to prevent it. And that move would be oblique. It was unlikely that Mellion Lee would move in on Gorjan directly. Russell had checked that the two men had never met, so that a call at the Hemmingway with good wishes or whisky would be excessively clumsy even for a diplomat. But somehow Lee must contact him, and it was Russell's guess that he would use the opening lying ready to his hand. For Mellion Lee's father owned a chain of newspapers. It varied from the frankly scandal-sheet to a weekly which liked to be considered a serious organ of serious opinion, but even the latter didn't lose too much money. Lee's father was an excellent business-man. So they'd ask for an interview, an exclusive probably, and they'd play it on from there. There were a dozen possibilities once contact had been made. Russell could block some of them or Palliser could block for him, but neither could prevent the original lead. Not for the first time Charles Russell would have to wait. Practice had made him good at it.

Nikola Mitrovic was less so. He had just received a tele-gram instructing him that Dr Gorjan was to give an exclusive interview to the representative of a chain of American news-papers, and his immediate emotion had been anger. Frustration too, since in the last resort it wasn't an instruction which he could query and hope to be listened to. He had made discreet inquiries from the Hemmingway Hospital and, though Alexan-der Gorjan wasn't anything like as well as he seemed to feel, no doctor had been prepared to say that an interview with a re-porter would actively endanger him. Several had tried already and on the ambassador's instructions had been turned away. But if His Excellency agreed that another be admitted there wasn't a medical reason to refuse him.

Nikola Mitrovic shook his head. He had less than Russell's information but he did have a nose for danger, and his instinct told him that the affair was of ill omen. Mitrovic wasn't afraid that Gorjan would give anything away—he was much too clever and much too well-disciplined; Mitrovic was afraid of he knew not what.

Which would cut no ice at home. To begin with he was in an awkward position personally, for he had just put up a formida-ble black. Starc's disappearance had been in most of the English papers and some of the speculation had been uncomfortably near the mark. And at home they would know the truth. They had impressed on Mitrovic that if Starc disappeared in Lon-don an invaluable lead would disappear with him, so the am-bassador was to hold the position quietly till the specialist in defectors could arrive to resolve it. But it hadn't worked out like that. Instead the embassy was on the horns since its official story was one of total ignorance why Starc should have chosen to absent himself. No other was possible publicly. Later they'd cook up something about some private trouble, debts probably or maybe a woman—anything that kept it purely personal. Mi-trovic's guess, like Palliser's, was that Starc would be out of the country, back with his damnable masters. But that was the last view he dared air publicly. Sooner or later he would have to talk to Russell again, but it was too early to take the initia-tive. Russell might add up two and two and Russell might then approach him. When he'd have to put his cards down. That depended on developments. Meanwhile his stock at home would certainly have slumped. There were excuses no doubt—

Petar simply hadn't been up to what had been asked of him—but excuses were very poor ground from which to challenge an instruction from the highest source. One Nikola Mitrovic might have been listened to. He doubted if they'd listen now.

In any case he could offer them nothing concrete. It was his instinct against the ineluctable facts of politics, and the latter were sharply against him. His country was communist but it wasn't a satellite, and it was a major interest of the West that it shouldn't become one. Much flowed from that, including money. Mostly it was given with a freedom which Mitrovic thought naïve, but he wasn't ignorant about the newspaper empire which had been specified in the instructions sent him. Which wasn't naïve at all. The senior Lee was a powerful man who could go to the top and talk there. Evidently he had done so. He would have said that with all those dollars propping the Confederacy surely it was outrageous that papers which earned their share of them should be treated like some London rag. And think of whom they rooted for. Mitrovic knew that the arguments wouldn't sound unreasonable and clearly they had been listened to. If he protested there would be pressures and counter-pressures, phone calls half across the world, more awkwardness for Mitrovic. Who simply couldn't afford it.

He groaned but he picked up the telephone. He'd have to explain to Gorjan.

Alexander Gorjan was feeling very well again. He was finding life in the decadent West unexpectedly pleasant. The hospital was comfortable, though the doctors who visited him seemed absurdly evasive, given to answers which weren't answers at all and to brisk bright smiles which annoyed him. But he could see that they knew their business, and when he tried to bully them they slapped him down firmly. He respected that and didn't resent it. He had unlimited books and wine within reason; his ambassador was visiting him and one or two hand-picked scientists. He had remembered now what had happened at the Circle but nobody had mentioned it. He was in no way ashamed —the old idiot had asked for it—but he genuinely hoped that he hadn't put his friends to too much trouble. A great many people had been extremely kind and he had found agreeable female company. Boredom, a lifelong enemy, was well below the horizon still: the books saw to that, the wine and the black nurse. Every day he felt stronger. The West, he decided, was treating him well, but he was a very important person now, not an unknown undergraduate. This was a capitalist society showing him its best side. That was how a communist must think, and after a lifetime he effortlessly did. So he was comfortable and recovering fast. Dialectic apart he might as well enjoy himself.

He was doing so as the telephone by his bedside interrupted

him. He rose from the armchair, pushing the nurse away, swearing softly. The oath had been a mild one for the call was no disaster. The nurse wouldn't leave him simply because a telephone had rung. He gave her a backward glance as he walked to the table. She had settled in the chair again. She looked half asleep and perhaps she was. She had a talent for sleep and others. He picked up the receiver.

'Alexander Gorjan? It's Mitrovic here.'

'It's kind of you to ring again.' They had been talking that morning.

'I hope you're going to think so. There's something I want you to do.'

'I doubt if I'm quite up to work. In a day or two perhaps——'

'It isn't exactly work. I want you to talk to a newspaper.'

'But you expressly warned me not to. I gather half a dozen have already tried. Your orders were to kick them out.'

'This is rather a special newspaper.'

'And why?'

Nikola Mitrovic said carefully: 'To begin with it isn't English.'

'I see. . . . At least I think I do. I imagine you've had instructions.'

'You could say I've had instructions—yes.'

'Then I suppose it's an interview. What sort of an interview?'

'Something they call a profile. I needn't say it won't be technical, and I've an undertaking you won't be asked about what happened at the Circle. A lot of personal background and some sentiment—you know the mixture. Your boyhood, the joys of Cambridge. Then work and ideals. Go easy on your hobbies, though. Oh, and the resorts along the coast aren't doing quite as well as we expected. Give them a push-along.'

'If that's what you really want.'

'We really want.' There was the faintest emphasis on 'We' and Gorjan caught it.

'All right. What day, what time?' Gorjan looked at the nurse. He knew her hours of duty and he didn't want to waste them.

'This evening. At six o'clock.'

'They sound in a hurry.'

'They pay for it if you follow me. And by the way, there's one bright spot. The interviewer's called Margaret Palfrey. That makes her a woman.'

Gorjan said contentedly: 'I've got one.'

Half an hour later a typescript translation was on Russell's desk. He read it smiling, remembering that only a few months ago a Minister had made a statement about wire-tapping. Russell had papers on the Member who had put down the Question and he could make a shrewd guess at which of his constituents had inspired it. The Minister had been reassuring and precise; he had given a modest figure and had stuck to it. Good luck to him. He had told the truth as he knew it since it was dangerous to do otherwise—the truth as he knew it or as Russell had allowed him to. Happily he had been hundreds wrong. Security was sufficiently difficult without having its hands tied by Members who sometimes meant well but more often were simply front men for the organizations which Russell was fighting. Charles Russell took risks but considered he was paid for it. Not particularly generously but he had accepted the terms. One of them was that he could be thrown to the wolves tomorrow. Nobody would defend him and he didn't expect it. There would be another hat on the elaborate bent-wood hatstand but the Executive wouldn't change much.

He read the report without surprise for it was much what he had expected. This was Move One, the approach by newspaper. So he'd guessed right so far, which was always reassuring, but he was puzzled by the choice of interviewer, a woman, Margaret Palfrey, and the name rang a bell: the Executive, he fancied, had a file on Margaret Palfrey. He sent for it and began to read.

The filing system in the Executive had only one equal and that was in Washington. Each file had a cover in one of three colours. Red was suspect by history or by positive association; green was suspect by known political sympathy; and yellow was suspect by character, mostly silly. Margaret Palfrey, once yellow, was now a green, and the summary was written in the style peculiar to the Executive, something between the aseptic impersonality of an entry in *Who's Who* and an obituary notice by a write-up man who had been given the sack unjustly and had resented it. But whatever the manner the *précis* on the left hand side was accurate. So, to her disadvantage, was the photograph:

MARGARET PALFREY. b. 11 August 1922, o.c. of Solomon Loeb of Manchester. Solomon Loeb was second generation English and made a good deal of money in cotton. In old age kind compatriots successfully parted him from most of it, but not before his daughter had had an excellent education. Lady Margaret Hall, where everybody expected her to get a First except her tutor. Later qualified as a doctor but never practised. Subsequently drifted into journalism, novels, broadcasting. Her actual position in that world is difficult to assess. Several novels which had some succès d'estime but no real sales which we have been able to discover. Is sufficiently well-considered in the snootier sort of journalism to interview the anti-novelist of the moment at a literary society, but her rate per written word we cannot guess (for means of livelihood, below). A Progressive with the largest capital available. Overt member of various organizations which plague us, and secret member of most others which do more, except the one which matters. Presumably discipline is distasteful.

Married (1) 1945, John Evans Carr, another doctor. Divorced her, minimum period. Wrote an unkind book about him. Married (2) February 1949, in Nigeria, one Charley Rosiji who (March 1949) took to the bush and stayed there. No book about that. Divorced him for desertion. Married (3) 1960, Richard Palfrey, aged 74, a retired Inspector of Taxes. Who was reputed to be fairly well off but had children by a previous marriage. Will was contested but unsuccessfully. Some honey for widow but very little. No issue by any union.

Has since lived on men and occasional fees from writing and broadcast criticism. Not important enough to be watched regularly, but some of her men are. A list of her known protectors is at Appendix A. But it is suggested that there have been other razors in the bathroom.

Charles Russell turned to Appendix A. It was a list of eight names and he read seven without surprise. The seven he could have guessed correctly—the fine flower of a world it was his business to know about. At the eighth he stopped abruptly, reading it again.

. . . Mr Mellion Lee of the American Embassy. That was something more than interesting, it was beginning to click together. Mellion Lee was known to dabble in what he would call the arts, and there were people who wouldn't have flinched from calling Margaret arty. No doubt it was unwise to have chosen a fellow-traveller as a mistress—there was something known as guilt by association—but perhaps he had never realized just how tarred with that brush she was. Or perhaps he had simply risked it. He was a very rich man and she still seemed attractive in her toothy, breasty way. In any case she would have handled him carefully, hiding what would have shocked him, deferring to what she would think of as his absurd provincial prejudices. And once you had a girl friend who was a literary journalist, what was more natural than to push a job her way, especially when on the face of it she looked a very good choice indeed? Gorjan was a communist, so you couldn't send just anyone to talk to him, somebody who might foam or freeze when the talk came round to communism. You'd have to choose with sympathy.

Charles Russell laughed aloud. That wouldn't have been bad reasoning but he knew it was mistaken. He had met enough communists to know one thing for certain: intellectual Lefties were beneath despising.

He lit a pipe, considering his counter-move. He hadn't one. He knew that a good many newspapers had been anxious to interview Gorjan and that none had been allowed to. Therefore this one had been, which meant there was a reason. Gorjan wouldn't have agreed without his ambassador's sanction, so clearly Mitrovic had given it. There could be guesses about why but they weren't, for the moment, helpful. Russell couldn't prevent this interview; he wasn't sure he wanted to. This was the opening, the original contact, but it was the developments which would be interesting.

So he'd still have to wait but there was one thing he ought to do. It was an axiom in the Executive to know your enemy, and if Alexander Gorjan wasn't precisely an enemy he was at least an essential actor. Russell had always wanted to meet him, and it wouldn't look extraordinary for a senior security officer to be paying a formal call on an important foreign visitor. In the Confederate Republic it was probably routine. But he couldn't just drop in on him; he'd have to clear with Mitrovic, to do the thing properly. He picked up his telephone, telling his secretary to get him the embassy. 'Say it's Charles Russell and I want to speak personally.'

Mitrovic was on the line at once. He said with a hint of anxiety: 'You'd like me to come and see you?'

'Not at the moment, thank you. But there's something you could do for me.'

'So?'

'I'd like to meet Dr Gorjan. Just a visit of courtesy.'

There was a moment of hesitation before Mitrovic said deliberately: 'You're not holding out on me? Nothing has happened?'

'Nothing to Gorjan. Did you expect it?'

His Excellency didn't answer but seemed satisfied. 'A visit of courtesy? That's really very kind of you.' There was a brief dry laugh. 'In any case I couldn't stop you. And I'm sure that you'll like him. When had you in mind?'

'I'm free at this moment.'

'He has an appointment this evening at six o'clock. I know because I fixed it. But I'll telephone now if that suits you.'

'I'd be very much obliged.'

Russell sent for his car, telling the driver to take him to the Hemmingway Hospital. He sat in the Humber happily, for meeting Gorjan was something he had been looking forward to. The more he read or heard of him the more he was attracted. Russell wasn't an anti-communist, or not in the sense that the word was a bogy. He was paid to frustrate the formidable apparatus of international communism, but it was an enemy which he feared and respected equally. There was arrogance here but at least there was decision. His hatred he saved for futile compromise, for the creaking bones of a calcified community. An

Anglo-Irishman, he could look at the English impersonally. What was contemptible about their establishment wasn't its power but its inefficiency. The supine respect for precedent, the passion for soldiers in fancy dress. The leather clubs and the squalid canteens. Industrial bigwigs talking on telly in terms of economics a generation out of date. Pompous trade unionists as startlingly antique. Compromise. Keep it clean. Russell had once told an eminent journalist that he was an old-fashioned radical. The man had blinked, then changed the subject. Russell had known he'd been misunderstood.

He ran up the steps of the Hemmingway, astonishingly agile for his sixty years. He filled in a form in duplicate, but smiling pleasantly, bottling his rage. An attendant took the forms away and, after ten minutes, another appeared. Russell went up in a lift with him, and on the landing there was a third attendant. There was a brief consultation, resentful and grudging. Clearly this was irregular and that was bad. But they'd had their instructions and that was worse. It was too early for regular visiting hours but they'd been told to admit him. Told! This was an imposition and they showed it. One of them nodded up the corridor. 'Number Ten,' he said sourly, 'left.' He didn't move to accompany Russell.

Russell walked along the corridor and knocked. Nobody answered. He knocked again, a little louder. Nothing again. He hesitated, then opened the door quietly, peeping in. There were two people there, one black one white, and neither had even noticed him.

A second later he was back in the corridor. He was conscious that he was blushing.

He blew his nose thoughtfully, then went downstairs again. He found his car and told the driver to take him to a modest pub in Egham. He had an appointment there with Oliver Copeman, and in a free and democratic country just twenty minutes left of drinking time. Copeman had been quietly planted in the Hemmingway, something between a nightwatchman and a handyman. By day there were other arrangements but Russell slept the sounder for the knowledge of Copeman at night. He was an admirable officer, resourceful and brave, and if he had a failing it was a certain stolidity; he liked a simple situation simply presented. . . . Tell him that you had just interrupted a scene you couldn't remember hindering since you'd turned a machine gun on a platoon of the Foreign Legion allegedly liberating a Sicilian village? Copeman would make a note of it; he wouldn't comment. Then tell him about Appendix A, eight gentlemen friends in fewer years. Hint that there had been casuals too. Then say that the lady would be calling on Gorjan at six. Who seemed to have made a remarkable recovery.

He seemed almost back to form again. . . . What form? Oh, never mind.

Copeman would make another note and then he'd ask for orders.

Fair enough, Russell thought—what orders? He'd been presented with a line—Gorjan, Margaret Palfrey, back to Mellion Lee. It was nothing very definite but he couldn't afford to lose it. Margaret Palfrey had an interview at six o'clock and it was Russell's opinion that it was likely to be protracted. But it mustn't be interrupted. A scene, for instance—people collecting, fuss. . . .

Lee would try something else and the Executive would be in the dark again. So there mustn't be a fuss—they couldn't risk it.

Russell walked into the private bar and Copeman rose to meet him. Russell bought drinks and they sat by the window and finished them. He bought more double whiskies, watching Copeman carefully. Copeman drank placidly, evidently enjoying it, but he didn't seem to mellow. Russell bought a final round, looking at his watch. Copeman saw him do it and said nothing. He'd been ordered to attend and he'd obeyed. Time was the boss's worry and meanwhile there was whisky. He'd never been tight on whisky in his life. At last Russell said: 'Will you be on duty at six o'clock?'

'Not exactly on duty. I come on at nine and go off at seven, but in practice I start much earlier. They think I'm after the overtime but in fact there's a gap.'

'A gap?'

'In cover, I mean—on Gorjan's room. The attendants keep civil service hours, which means they go off at five or five-thirty, and the nurse leaves at six. There's a night nurse for the wards of course, but in the bigwigs' corridor they don't lay one on unless it's necessary. Now Gorjan's much better so he only has a day nurse. A blackie, she is, and very nice too.'

'So I gathered.'

'Sir?'

'Never mind. So you patrol Gorjan's corridor?'

Copeman said cautiously: 'I wouldn't say patrol, sir. I've work to do, the boilers and so on, but I do keep an eye on it. Regularly.'

'Nobody else would be around at six?'

'It's very unlikely. Supper comes up at seven.'

An hour, Russell thought—that would be plenty. 'There's a lady calling on Dr Gorjan at six.'

Copeman asked sharply: 'She's dangerous?'

'Not to Gorjan, or not directly. But she's important to us—a lead. I don't want to lose it and we might if there's a scene.'

'A scene, sir?'

'An interruption.'

'Then what do you want me to do?'

'Precisely nothing.'

Oliver Copeman made a note in a neat leather pocket book. Russell peeped at it unashamed. It read simply: DO NOTHING. Russell said suddenly: 'I imagine you think I'm mad.'

'Oh no sir, not at all, sir.'

'I wouldn't dare blame you. Listen Copeman, you may hear sounds of a scuffle, cries. Cries for help.'

'Cries for help, sir. Yes, sir.'

'Pitiful female cries. Later the cries will diminish. Other sounds will replace them. Cries again but different. Are you a married man?'

'I am.'

'If I may ask it—happily?'

'Four children and one coming, sir.'

'Then I make myself clear?'

'You do.'

CHAPTER 6

Margaret Palfrey drove from the Hemmingway to Mellion Lee's flat in the car which he had lent her. She hadn't been there often, for Lee never asked her when he had diplomatic or business friends. She knew he had the rich man's itch to live in more worlds than one, the professional man's caution in keeping them well apart. She wasn't surprised and she wasn't resentful; she privately admired his solid sense. Mellion Lee was too intelligent not to see through the world of painters covering canvas on a salary from a dealer, the world of slim volumes published at the poet's own expense. A foot in what was spurious amused him; he could always pull out of it and one day he would. That was what he told himself but Margaret knew him better. This was a substitute though not for success, since as Counsellor of Embassy Lee wasn't unsuccessful. But it depended how you used the word. Another man might envy Lee but never a woman. Mellion shouldn't have been born rich for he'd have been happy making money. Making his own way would have fulfilled him. Perhaps that was the key to him. Mellion Lee was a diplomat but his talents weren't diplomatic. Such a life, for a Lee, could be dangerously frustrating. One day he'd break in surprising action. Not, she was sure, as Stevan had— knifed in some brawl he'd declined to explain, then disappearing in hate and contempt. They were violent these Slavs, but men. She thought for a moment of Alex Gorjan, smiling a little shyly. Alex and Stevan had something in common, nothing with Mellion Lee.

And where did she herself come in? As a woman she didn't.

Keeping a mistress proved something. Not what he wished to prove, but part of it.

He poured her a drink and sat down. 'Could I see your notes, please?'

She considered him as he read them. He wasn't bad-looking in his hungry way. His hair had gone grey but he still kept all of it, and he hadn't an ounce of fat on him. He had always been very generous. Of course! A Lee couldn't risk the appearance that he was tight with cash, much less that he was short of it. Unexpectedly the thought shamed her. He wasn't God's gift to a woman of forty but he'd never put a hand wrong. That at least had been a change for her. He now said warmly: 'But these are very good indeed. Congratulations.'

'Thank you.'

He was silent again and she didn't interrupt him. He had a deliberate mind and he liked to concentrate: break in on his thinking and he'd flare in irritation. He was thinking that the affair was going well. A very important visitor to London, a friend of his father, had sent for him and had talked about Alex Gorjan. The visitor had been discreet but his basic intention obvious. Gorjan was in England and the English weren't exactly notable for seeing an opportunity and exploiting it. But if he could be persuaded to come to America. . . . Yes, persuaded. This wasn't a job for You Know What. You Know What was in the doghouse. And naturally success would be a considerable feather in Lee's cap. He'd been left in London rather a long time, and it was the visitor's impression that promotion and a better post wouldn't be hard to arrange.

. . . So persuasion, as I said, though of course there were several sorts of it. Well, there you are. Good luck.

Lee hadn't been tempted by the prospect of promotion, indeed he had hidden a private smile at the innocence which assumed it. In fact he'd come near the dusty end of work which had never absorbed him. But though he wasn't ambitious as a diplomat he shared the prejudices of his trade. And the chief was to fear the Agency. He had flown back to Washington a few months before and the drawing-rooms had been buzzing waspishly. It was intolerable that policy should apparently be made by an organization responsible to nobody. . . . But it was? Well, in theory maybe, but no one would think so. Important conferences wrecked by some aircraft where it shouldn't have been, a half-trained gang of cutthroats whipped off a target it should never have been allowed on. Not that quite everyone agreed. Lee had been running the fashionable line and had earned himself a snub he wasn't used to. It had been a very old gentleman and he had listened with the patience of the old. . . . Had Mr Lee finished what he wished to say? He had? Then he would permit him to put on record that

Mr Lee was an ass. The old gentleman had been acid and he had used a most frightening word. These opinions were un-American and for two bits he'd report them. If he had needed two bits.

Mellion Lee had discovered he didn't. Lee had a proper respect for money and the old gentleman's money was even bigger than his own. Moreover it was older. The gaffe had annoyed him but it hadn't changed his mind. Old fogies might speak for the Agency still—why, they even seemed grateful. But good citizens must clip its too potent wings.

Mellion Lee rose thoughtfully, pouring more drinks. Back in his chair he said: 'Then it went off all right with Gorjan?'

'Yes, I liked him.'

'Do you think he liked you?'

'I'm sure.'

'Then I shall follow this up. I'd like you to introduce me to Gorjan. I'll cable your article as soon as you've finished it and we'll say that my father was so impressed he insisted on my meeting him.'

'Won't it look a bit odd?'

'Perhaps, but I can ride it. I'll go on about my father. I'll say he's a tyrant and wouldn't take no.'

He was, Lee thought, at that. His father was ashamed of him—diplomacy didn't produce things. One day he'd show him.

'But why do you want to meet Gorjan?'

For a moment she saw him hesitate. 'I'm going to ask him to the cottage.'

'Whatever for?' Margaret Palfrey was astonished. Gorjan was a communist and Lee an American. There was much which she must hide from him herself. She said again: 'What for?'

'We've business to discuss, that's all.'

Margaret concealed a sardonic smile. She was remembering he was a diplomat and they loved their little mysteries. 'And how will you fix the visit?'

'In the same way I fixed your interview. Through Father.'

Margaret Palfrey went sourly silent. God, what a world. A very rich country and rather a poor one. A newspaper proprietor, his papers supporting the Administration of the moment, close to the big men. . . . She wasn't surprised by what Lee told her since it fitted her preconceptions. That was how they ran things. . . . Not for much longer.

But he was speaking again. 'And I'd like you to come down too.' Unmistakably it had been an instruction. Margaret Palfrey thought of herself as the contemporary free woman and a free woman must at once resent an order. She said coolly: 'You would?'

'I would.'

'If you're thinking of the doctoring I'm hardly that now. Suppose he has another stroke?'

47

'You'll be plenty good enough for what I want.'

She looked at him quickly, suddenly attentive. She had never met his father but had often imagined him. This might have been his father's voice. She said, quietly watching him: 'You sound very sure.'

'I am.'

Now she was staring. This was a Mellion Lee she'd never seen.

Margaret Palfrey had left Gorjan with an emotion which would have surprised her if she had known it. She had made him a little homesick. It wasn't his habit to count his amorous successes, and if it had been Margaret wouldn't have rated. Margaret Palfrey had been too easy to be recorded as a serious achievement, and as a woman she had annoyed him. For he had seen through her at once. The leftish banalities, the facile sympathy too lushly offered—these were the West at its worst.

He began to think of the Confederate Republic. It would be good to be back at work again, and good to play. There was a breakthrough which he had almost made and he knew it could be important—used. The soldiers would be delighted and the politicians more. Then a week on the beach with a woman who was one, trips into the mountains in his new Italian car. There was only one in the country, for foreign exchange was precious still. He smiled but without complacency. He'd more than earned his Maserati.

Yes, he'd like to get back to work again; he'd like to go home. He had raised it with Mitrovic that morning and Mitrovic hadn't answered. Gorjan hadn't pressed him: after all he'd had a very full programme in his intended week in England, and though it was unlikely that the whole could be restored it was possible that one or two engagements would be worth rearranging. Nikola had explained that he was asking for instructions and he'd casually let slip that the doctors were pleased with their patient. But they were English doctors, not men to be rushed, and they'd have to be quite sure before discharging him. . . . How long would that be? Nikola Mitrovic had grinned. He'd done many things in an active life but doctoring hadn't been one of them.

Alexander Gorjan yawned and stretched. He was pleasantly tired but not exhausted. Better still he wasn't bored yet though he knew that soon he might be. Perhaps if they wouldn't discharge him yet they'd let him go out on ticket of leave. A long weekend. He'd go up to Cambridge and potter around. Mitrovic could fix it if the doctors agreed, but he'd sound them himself before embarrassing Nikola unnecessarily. He'd talk to the psychiatrist. He was more than a little phoney but he wasn't unintelligent, and if the proper doctors disliked the idea it was certain a psychiatrist would press it.

Gorjan drank some wine and read for an hour. He then went to sleep. Life wasn't intolerable if you knew how to handle it.

Charles Russell was drinking sherry in his club when Normer of Nowhere came up to him. That wasn't his style and title but it had stuck. He was a scientist who had properly been ennobled for outstanding work on radar, but he hadn't fancied a territorial title derived from territory he had never held. So, since he had been born there, he had suggested Lord Tooting Bec. This hadn't gone down well. For one thing there had been a music-hall song about Tooting Bec—an elderly Herald could remember it verbatim—and for another Tooting wasn't considered euphonious. The future peer was a first-class scientist but hardly an enthusiast for the niceties of nobility. He had told them to toss up for it and presumably somebody had. He had a handle now but it amused him to forget it. He was Normer of Nowhere and secretly rather proud of it. No feudal halfwit bore arms as ancient.

He walked up to Russell openly, holding a quart of beer. He had a beer-drinker's stomach but was happily resigned to it. Across the silver tankard he said easily: 'Let's go into the library.'

Russell followed him at once. He looked round the splendid room, seeing that it was empty. When they were settled Normer asked bluntly: 'Tell me why Gorjan's here.'

'He came for the Andover Lecture.'

'Tchah!'

'It happens to be the truth you know. He then had that breakdown and they took him to hospital. I can tell you what he's doing there—he's trying to get well again. For a man who lives as he does that's a job in itself.'

'You don't want to play ball with me?' Normer didn't sound offended.

'I didn't say that or mean to imply it. You're Lord Normer— I trust you.'

'Thanks.' Lord Normer took a swig of beer, suppressing a belch but not too severely. 'I've been wondering, you see. I work in the world of microwaves, what you mostly call radar. In fact it's far wider—far. The Iron Curtain isn't called that for nothing, but there's still a sort of grapevine between top-class scientists. If I may include myself. It isn't what we hear but what we don't. We know where we stand ourselves and we can often deduce where the other chap doesn't. It may not sound much to a layman but you'd be surprised where it takes us. And where it takes me at the moment is that Gorjan must be near to something big. And I was one of the people detailed to go down to the hospital and talk to him. Of course I didn't try to pump him but there was something about him'— Lord Normer waved his beer—'a glow, I don't know, I suppose this sounds rubbish, but when you're really on to something, when you're blissfully stuck in. . . . You can't mistake it. Like —like a woman with a lover.'

'It doesn't sound rubbish.'

'I'm glad. Not that I believe he's got a secret—not in the sense of science fiction. If he had that sort of secret, and there are precious few left, they'd never have let him leave the country. I don't quite believe you about the Andover Lecture but I can guess at your inhibitions. It's not important. I'm not telling you that he and he alone knows the secret of some schoolboy paper's ray; I'm saying that in the world of micro-waves I believe he's ahead of the rest of us. It might be almost anything—I told you the field was enormous.'

'You wouldn't care to cut it down?'

'I'll *guess* it down—remember that.' Normer stared at his empty quart and Russell rang for a waiter. While the beer was arriving Normer went on reflectively: 'People tend to think of missiles as things which go up and down—motor at one end, warhead the other, and some sort of homing system sand-wiched in the middle. But it doesn't work out as simply, es-pecially with the big ones. Guidance systems were always pretty complicated and interference has made them more so. I know of four proven methods of upsetting a missile's targeting, but so does everybody else. So they build four anti-interference systems into what's already a considerable mass of electronic gear. It's already a serious problem. You can't cut the fuel for a given range, and cutting the warhead is self-defeating. But the bit between motor and warhead gets steadily more complicated, so, given your limitations, the missile itself gets bigger and bigger. The Big Boys, the Inter-Continentals, are pretty well near the limit now.'

'So that a fifth means of interference, a really new one——'

'It would be countered of course—in time. Somebody would untangle it, and another enormously sophisticated piece of elec-tronics would be built into your rocket. If, as I say, the thing could still be done and make it fly. But that apart there's the question of time. So far this interference has been more or less move and counter-move. And counter-counter-move. We've known something about Alpha, so Alpha-Beta hasn't caught us entirely napping and we've developed Alpha-Gamma fairly quickly. So back we are at Alpha again. But something, as you call it, really *new*——'

Russell said slowly: 'What would it mean?'

'Militarily? The balance of terror? It would depend who you were.'

'Go on.'

'Suppose you had to fire them first. Suppose that even ten per cent fell harmlessly in the Arctic. I know that doesn't sound a lot, but remember that your first targets won't be cities but the means of retaliation. It won't perhaps deter you that your enemy suffers less but there'll also be certain knowledge that your own side will suffer more. That's what bridge players call a swing, you know—you count it both ways.'

Russell was silent, for he'd heard this before. That had been from Palliser but Palliser wasn't a scientist. He asked at length: 'And that's your guess?'

'It isn't melodramatic and it doesn't offend what's known. You could call it an informed guess.'

'Which Gorjan holds the answer to, or very soon may?'

'I think so—yes.'

'Then coming from where he comes from—would you like to be Gorjan?'

'That's what I came to tell you. . . . No.'

CHAPTER 7

Charles Russell, as usual, had had eight hours' untroubled sleep, and with that behind him he was facing a decision next morning. An eminent American was on record that it was easier to put a microphone into a man's room than a girl into his bed, but that had been the voice of expertise. Russell didn't quite credit that Mellion Lee had sent his mistress to Gorjan with express instructions to seduce him: that less aseptic method was admittedly an amateur's, but it didn't sound like Lee at all. In any case his motives were much less interesting than the results of action. Lee had arranged an interview and would be delighted that it had been successful. As Russell was sure it had. Lee wouldn't ask for details but he'd certainly seize an advantage. The next move might come in days not weeks. Charles Russell frowned. These damned *dilettanti*, rushing their assignments. . . .

It was time he talked to somebody who spoke the same language he did. There was a transatlantic Agency of matchless resources and competence and Russell and its London head could talk as established equals. This was a time to do so.

He sent for a taxi, not his car, directing it to a house in Park Crescent, climbing out briskly, paying the driver from the silver he always carried. On the pavement he looked around him. This was Good Works-land, Councils for this and Institutes for that. There was even a Foundation. The inhabitants were recognizable across a room, men and women of the highest principles. Russell had nothing against them provided they weren't obliged to meet, and in this graceful Crescent they had at least been intelligent. There were salaries here which they couldn't have earned in the competitive world outside it. What mattered here was Service. Profit and loss were vulgar words.

Russell walked along the Crescent, quietly admiring it. A superior young woman had once explained to him that speculative building wasn't excused by being admirably designed. They had met at some party and Russell had smoothly slipped her, since she hadn't been pretty enough to compensate for views which bored him. Not, he thought now, that she hadn't been right. The bombing had exposed that these houses were jerry-built, but Russell forgave that easily. He had just been down to the Hemmingway Hospital, and after that barbarity there was an inescapable word for Park Crescent. It mightn't be conscientious but at least it was civilized.

He walked through a door up a flight of stairs which pleased him. On the landing were other doors, and on one of them a bright brass plate—The Milton Export and Import Company. Russell pushed the door open and in a second had crossed the Atlantic. The room he now stood in was decently warm, and if anyone drank tea there they had put away the cups. There were two clerks at businesslike desks, a receptionist and, in a corner behind another desk, a sharp-eyed young man in a suit which wasn't English. There was an air of brisk prosperity which Russell approved. This was a front and he happened to know it. But nobody else would. The Milton was a genuine business genuinely paying its way. He took out a visiting card, giving it to the receptionist. 'I'd like to see Mr Scobell, please.'

'Have you an appointment, sir?'

'No, but I hope he'll see me.'

'I'm afraid he's in conference. If I could ring you. . . .'

The sharp-eyed young man had risen and crossed the room. He looked at Russell's card and then at Russell; he bowed politely. 'Colonel Russell? I've always wanted to meet you.' He inspected Russell levelly and without impertinence, then said surprisingly, almost to himself: 'A legend walking in on us.' His manner changed again abruptly. 'If you'd please come with me, sir.' He led the way to another door and opened it. As Russell walked past he announced him formally: 'Colonel Charles Russell of the Security Executive.'

He went away.

A man behind a large clear desk had already risen. Russell had told his Minister that he liked his Americans American and this one was authentic. His hair was black, untouched by grey, though he was almost as old as Russell, and there was a hint of powder round a considerable but well-shaved jowl. James Scobell was as different from Mellion Lee as two men of the same race could be. Where Lee was thin and English-elegant Scobell looked like the tackle he once had been. Where Lee talked Boston with overtones of an Oxford that never was, Scobell had a fine western whine which it had never occurred to him to mitigate. His vocabulary, yes: on his last trip home they'd laughed at him. But never the whinny. He said in it now: 'Will you have a cigar?'

'One of yours—certainly.'

Russell lit the cigar with ritual care. Scobell was already smoking. He said through a reflective cloud: 'It must be important to bring you here. Yourself, I mean.'

'Yes, I trust my own telephone and I've guaranteed yours.' Russell made a sitting bow. 'Courtesy of the profession. But I wanted to talk personally—frankly to watch you as well as listen. I don't quite know how you'll be taking this.'

'We've always played ball when our employers allowed us.'

'And sometimes when they didn't?'

James Scobell said deliberately: 'I hear the words.'

'That's good enough to start with.' Russell blew smoke at the handsome ceiling. 'Then you'll have heard of Alexander Gorjan.'

'Who's in this country now, who threw a bottle at old Merridew and got him. Who then had a nervous breakdown and was taken to the Hemmingway.'

'Where the night he arrived two agents tried to murder him.'

'Is that so?' Scobell sounded interested but he didn't look surprised. He wasn't easily astonished.

'Did you know he was *sent* here—deliberately removed from the Confederate Republic by his own authorities?'

'No, I didn't know that, but now you tell me I believe you. We know how hot things are out there, and Gorjan's a party man. The *existing* party. He's also the biggest radar man alive.' Scobell shrugged his tackle's shoulders. 'And so——'

'So they sent him to England, where he damned near gets murdered.'

'But doesn't. Of course that was thanks to you. Fraternal congratulations.' Scobell grinned amiably. 'You see I've picked up a little English in my time here. I've also picked up a great respect for a Colonel Charles Russell. So where do *I* come in? If you mean me to, that is. If I'm not jumping you.'

'No.' Russell looked at his cigar, apparently intent on it. 'Do you know Mellion Lee?' He was looking at Scobell now, not his ash. James Scobell was expressionless but he was thinking. He said at length: 'Put another card down, please. Just one. I'll play with you when I've seen it.'

'Then Mellion Lee seems inexplicably interested in Alexander Gorjan.'

'Inexplicably? I don't think so.' James Scobell shook his head. 'We're a peculiar people—I've learnt that since I've been here. We like to think of ourselves as great inventors but in practice we're not. What we are is great improvers, great developers. Better mousetraps, you know, not the mousetrap originally. And we hate to see resources wasted. Gorjan is a major radar man, and for one reason or another he's now this side of the Iron Curtain. Your side to be accurate, but I reckon I know how your minds work. You wouldn't move to exploit him yourselves. You'd see all the difficulties and I'm not denying them. There would be political complications you couldn't see the end of and the sheer human decencies of not hunting a sick man. We'd see those too but they wouldn't be decisive. To any good American Gorjan would be temptation.'

"I'd got as far as that myself but it's not the whole story. Here's Mellion Lee, a Counsellor of Embassy, contacting Gorjan. Why Mellion Lee?' Russell leant forward. 'Now if it had been yourself——'

'I can't answer that one.'

No, Russell thought, he couldn't. Nor did he need to. The Milton Export and Import Company hid the operations branch in London of one of the most powerful organizations in the world. Russell blessed his God that it existed, but in the past few months it had run into a streak of mostly undeserved bad luck, and in Security, Intelligence if you preferred it, it was the last result which counted. You could spirit away the heads of your enemy's bureaus, acquiring from what they told you more than your own agents could discover in a lifetime; you could dig a sensational tunnel, tapping a hostile communications system for months and years on end; and all this would count for nothing when you really dropped a big one. Fly an aircraft on an authorized mission but see it suffer the misfortune of a flame-out, advise that an invasion was a fair military risk when in fact it was a gamble. . . . Heads would roll fast and had. Besides, there had to be a scapegoat for there were new men now in power. Russell wouldn't mention that. Scobell was a good Republican, a man of few words and brief ones. He'd say something about a gang of Boston micks, and later he would regret it, for he was an American first and Russell wasn't. What mattered at the moment was that he was a professional who'd been by-passed: a job he should have handled had been given to an amateur. Russell thought it stupid but the fact remained. The reasons too and he knew them to be bad ones. Politics and Intelligence did not mix. Above all things mistrust was fatal.

Well, the boys would grow up; they'd learn from their mistakes in time but this one would be in England. That was why Russell had called at the Milton. On a note of inquiry he said again: 'Mr Mellion Lee. . . .'

'You probably know his background already, but I'll recite. He started as a mathematician—I mean he took an excellent degree in mathematics. I gather he meant to stay on and teach but he never did. The war came along, the Navy turned him down for the typically Navy reason that he was only slightly colour blind, and I suspect that before he really knew what hit him the State Department had made its grab. And there he's stayed. He's been successful enough but I doubt if he's a happy man.'

'Whatever he is he's worked himself in on this one. So it's going to be Embassy Intelligence.'

Scobell smiled wryly. 'Is that what you call it? We've a rougher word here.'

'Then how do you see it breaking?'

'How's it gone so far?'

'You'll know about Lee's father's newspapers. Gorjan gave an interview to one of them last night. Mellion Lee must have fixed it since every other paper has been refused.'

'Very slick lead-in.' Scobell nodded approvingly. 'Who did they send?'

'A Mrs Margaret Palfrey.'

'Hell.'

'You know Mrs Palfrey?'

'Sure I know her. She's an addlepate Leftie and she's Mellion Lee's mistress. She's also something else you'll have a word for—not mine perhaps but it means the same. Just how far Left she is I doubt if Lee knows. But I do.' James Scobell was relaxed but with the unmistakable authority of long experience. 'That's the rod I keep in pickle, friend, and how it would pickle the diplomats! Counsellor of Embassy living with fellow-travelling nymph. . . . They'd do most things to muffle that one. I don't know Lee well enough to wish him ill, but I need something like that just in case the embassy starts getting in our hair. At the moment I don't grade Lee higher than a striped pants under orders, but in this game you never know. They're a formidable family in any case.'

'You're remarkably far-sighted.' Russell spoke admiringly but Scobell shrugged.

'I pick up what's offered me.'

'Cutting me in?'

'Whenever I can. And you've spared me the awkward questions. Shoot.'

'Then how do you see it developing?'

'Messy and maybe dangerous—for all of us pros. Lee stinks of money and there's what he calls a cottage for weekends. That's a ready made set-up so he'll probably try to use it. And why not? If Lee has strings enough to fix an exclusive interview he'll also have the pull to get approval for a visit. So if the doctors will stand for it he'll try to get Gorjan to stay with him. Mrs Palfrey as go-between, maybe as bait.' James Scobell smiled but not with amusement. 'Convalescence, they'll call it.'

'And in fact?' Russell asked.

'A God-awful bungle. I can only guess at what they'll try, but whatever it is it won't succeed. Probably they'll try bribery—no, not money directly. They're not that stupid. They'll talk about the American way of life, show him pictures of plushy houses, hunting trips in the mountains. All the kingdoms of the world and he won't give a damn. He's a commie and a good one. The one thing that might tempt him they simply won't think of. Do you know what that is?'

Charles Russell shook his head.

'The best laboratory in the world. An unlimited budget quite without strings. Work on anything he fancies whether it's useful militarily or not. He's a top-grade scientist and I know my scientists.'

'You seem to. And when they've fallen down on the American way of life?'

'They'll work on him all right, but it's guessing how. Things they've read in books, perhaps. Frame him in a card game, threaten to make a fuss——'

'Corn,' Russell said.

'The tallest. . . . Any other ideas?'

'A dozen, all futile. I'm inclined to agree he'll laugh at them, but supposing he doesn't. I don't mean they'll ever tempt him but he's still sicker than he seems. Suppose he takes it badly, has another breakdown and——'

'It's your country, Colonel. Your worry.'

Russell said reflectively: 'I'd like a man in that cottage.'

'As it happens, so should I, though for rather different reasons. I can't work against my own embassy, or at any rate not until we're forced to pick their bits up. We haven't quite got to that yet, so I'm obliged to play it carefully. Just the same I'd like to minimize the mess and I've been thinking how to do it. A good reliable man in that cottage was as far as I'd got around to.'

'If you'd rather have your own good man——'

'No, I'd rather have yours. We've an interest in common so I'll make you a proposition.'

'Make it a good one.'

'The best. We've done some spadework, and this so-called cottage is a long way from a town. It's difficult to get help there and they badly need a handyman. I had just the one to plant on them but instead I'll plant yours. If we need to, that is—if Gorjan does go down there. Your side of the bargain will be to pass me what this ear-man tells you. He'll be working for you but you'll share the news with me. The news and no more, for I don't mean to blunder in. Okay?'

'I'm very much obliged to you.' Russell hadn't hesitated.

'You're welcome.' Scobell rose with Russell and shook hands. As Russell went through the door he said: 'Good luck to us.'

'I've a hunch we're going to need it.'

The two white-coated men were sitting in the senior's room at the Hemmingway Hospital. The man behind the desk was a physician and perhaps a little conscious that the other was not. The psychiatrist was ineluctably a mid-European and the Scot didn't like him. He had often told himself that this was prejudice, but he was too intelligent to believe that prejudices were necessarily disgraceful. Besides the other came of a race which could do anything but behave with discretion and he wasn't, at the moment, talking notably tactfully. In his throaty rasp he was saying pontifically: 'In my considered opinion——'

'Yes?' The cool northern voice was polite but deadly.

The psychiatrist swallowed noisily, changing in an instant to what was almost obsequiousness.

'A few days in the country would do Gorjan good. Mr Lee has been kind enough to make that possible.'

'Then you know Mr Lee? It was you he approached, I think.'

'I know him slightly, yes. I'm interested in the arts, you see, and there's a place we both belong to.'

'The arts, yes of course.' It didn't sound a dirty word, only one suspect to practical men.

'And my brother has a gallery where Mr Lee sometimes buys.' The psychiatrist was pleased with that: that at least was business.

'I see. And the proposal now is that Gorjan should visit Lee for a long weekend?'

The other nodded and the physician was silent. The invitation struck him as unusual but not so unusual that it was easy to object to it. Mellion Lee's father was a newspaper tycoon and the Lees, presumably using their diplomatic strings, had arranged that an eminent patient should give an exclusive interview to one of the father's newspapers. It had probably been some shameless fix but that wasn't a doctor's concern. So up comes a woman to the Hemmingway and the interview had been a long one. The doctor knew that because its length had begun to worry him; he had almost gone to Gorjan's room, but he was a Scot and shy, and he hadn't been able to think of an excuse which sounded reasonable. He couldn't afford to look a fool nor risk the appearance of vulgar prying. But he had seen the woman leave. She had been walking very lightly, bright as a sparrow, and when she had gone he had visited his patient. Gorjan had been quieter than usual, looking a little fatigued. The doctor had shrugged. He knew nothing about the world of newspapers but was determined that nothing should surprise him. If that was the technique for very exclusive interviews. . . .

Then back comes the woman next day with Mellion Lee, introducing him boldly and with a reasonable story. Lee senior had been so impressed with the interview, so impressed with the man who could give it, that he felt his son must meet him. If the doctor would agree, of course. They had both been entirely correct and it had been equally difficult to refuse them. One interview with a stranger had already been allowed and a second wasn't easy to distinguish. Gorjan wasn't ill, or not in the sense that a visit would upset him, but he could have another attack tomorrow, in which case he'd probably die. That was the risk but it was wholly unpredictable.

It was the unpredictability which was worrying the chief physician of the Hemmingway. He wasn't a self-important man, and he didn't resent that Lee had gone directly to the psychiatrist, not himself. After all they'd been acquainted, the psychiatrist had informed him, and the invitation which had followed wasn't medically outrageous. A few days in the country might indeed do Gorjan good. He'd been asking about it himself and patients weren't always wrong. Gorjan had suggested Cambridge but this would be quieter. Gorjan at the moment was almost well. He stood in a shadow but it could engulf him anywhere—in the Hemmingway or a country house, you couldn't do more than guess it. This looked all right and it probably was.

An instinct said insistently it wasn't.

The doctor returned to the man across his desk. He took from a drawer the chart of an encephalogram, passing it to the other. 'What do you make of that?'

'The human brain. . . . I've a limited faith in machinery when applied to it.'

'No doubt.' The physician was succinct but still polite.

'But I don't deny facts. Doctor, Gorjan is still disturbed.'

'We've not much in common then. My own opinion, for what it's worth, is that if he were anyone else but who he is it would be our duty to call a surgeon. There's pressure—I'm convinced of it.'

The psychiatrist said contemptuously: 'A butcher.' He was arrogant again and the doctor detested him.

'The word in this room is surgeon. Not that it's important since they'd never let us operate.'

'Then all that is left us is civilized treatment. Relaxation in the country would be part of it.'

'Perhaps.'

'Do you forbid it?' The psychiatrist hadn't intended it but the sentence came out as a snarl. He was an arrogant man but not a brave one and it had cost him an effort to utter it. A man surer of himself, more certain of his profession, could have dropped it out lightly, almost as jest between equals. In the mouth of this expatriate the words were a naked threat.

The doctor was silent again. He was beaten and knew it. He had only his instinct to set against a proposal which at the worst was innocuous and might be beneficial. Besides, he wasn't the final court. He knew that the interview with Gorjan had been arranged through his ambassador, for an Excellency had telephoned himself. So the ambassador must have approved this visit too. If some doctor impeded it they'd start making it pretty hot for him, bringing in consultants, ringing the Board of Management. . . .

The physician rose stiffly and walked to the open window. Out of it he said sadly: 'I don't much like it but——'

'But what?'

'Oh, take him away.'

'Oh, take him away' were the only words not quite clear on the tape which Charles Russell was playing back two hours later. But they were clear enough. Copeman had been busy and effectively, and the doctor would have had to be very experienced to find the microphone even if he had known that one was hidden. Russell reversed the recorder, playing the tape a second time.

. . . So it wasn't Gorjan's body now, it was Alexander Gorjan alive. The hounds were at his heels again and Russell resented the trespass. Not killers now, the ruthless tools of a policy aiming simply at erasement: they wanted a scientist's mind, his will; they wanted the power to use him. In their different way they were just as lethal. Gorjan had been very sick, and moreover he was a guest. So, for that matter was this bloody Lee, shamelessly abusing a mild host's house. Russell cursed quietly, suppressing a mounting anger. He reached for the telephone, giving his secretary a number which wasn't in the Directory under the Milton Export and Import Company. . . . Yes, exactly as you forecast. Mellion Lee had followed up the interview and Gorjan was to stay with him for a long weekend. Mitrovic must have agreed again, why was an open guess, but at least it served his original purpose which was keeping Gorjan in England. So this man of mine, this man of *ours*. . . . Yes, right away. Name Oliver Copeman and wholly competent. Tonight? To Scobell's house? Understood and agreed.

Russell lit a reflective pipe. The affair looked well enough in hand except for Starc, and Starc wasn't his urgent pigeon. Palliser had done rather more than hint at that and Russell had been grateful. Diplomats were indeed dangerously explosive properties often better left alone. Two men were under interrogation still and they could scarcely be less than interesting. All information was interesting, the Executive thrived on it. They might or might not know if Starc had a hideout— Russell was inclined to think they wouldn't—and they might or might not disclose it. But as things stood the knowledge could be at least as embarrassing as useful.

If Starc were still there.

Colonel Russell sat upright suddenly. Palliser had seen it as a simple alternative: either Starc had been whisked away or Starc was in hiding and would remain so until discovered. Which had been logical thinking from civilized premises. Unhappily Starc's masters weren't in that sense civilized. There was a third course open with an agent who had failed. If you couldn't get him out or didn't want to, if he wasn't worth saving but was still a risk at large. . . .

There was a well-established method with blown agents such as these.

Charles Russell frowned for he hated murder.

CHAPTER 8

Stevan Starc had always seen his own position with brutal clarity. There had been a moment when, with a valid passport and the two hundred pounds he always kept in cash, he could have walked out of England openly, but it was too late now for that. In any case he had never seriously considered it. Two hundred pounds wouldn't last for long and he had no fancy to join the nameless army of ex-agents, blown to both sides, useful to neither, eternally on the run. He knew that his future lay inescapably with his masters; and he knew his masters' mind. They wouldn't look after him from any sense of loyalty —they simply didn't think like that; they'd pull him out of England if they considered him worth the pulling or if the risk of leaving him was one which they couldn't accept. But that risk could be avoided by other means than obliging him, and Stevan Starc well knew it. Four days had gone by and there hadn't been a message. He was almost without hope and he was beginning to be afraid.

But not that the police would find him easily. His hideout was a good one and the police wouldn't pull the stops out for just another missing person. There was Petar of course, a small matter of mayhem, but Petar wouldn't identify him without Mitrovic's sanction, and Mitrovic had pressing political reasons not to wash his soiled linen publicly. There was the barmaid too—the Bear and Staff. Almost certainly they'd nose her out and she wouldn't last five minutes. But the worst she could make him was an accredited diplomat who'd been sending dubious messages to the shadier of his compatriots, for he'd never dared trust them with anything that mattered. He'd been keeping them together as potentially useful, feeding them the odd jobs; they would now be picked up but they'd always been expendable. When he'd needed a man for serious work he had had to import two good ones.

Who had simply disappeared and that did matter.

Starc had considered that aspect too. Part of his training had been a summary of the English legal system, and it had been presented to him with a mixture of incredulity and contempt—the preposterous shackles it fettered on proper police work, the insistence on evidence, even proof, the laughable assumption that a man must be innocent until somebody proved him guilty. That meant that in the world of espionage an agent had advantages which almost no other country offered him. Starc had been taught to think against this background and had done so. Two men would crack, linking him with attempted murder, but there wouldn't be the evidence to lay before some judge, nor even the sort of case the police must insist on closing.

No, but there was the Security Executive. They might already be suspecting him, making the long guesses of experience, but confront them with confirmation that he'd planned the attempt on Gorjan and at once he'd cease to be the mysteriously disappearing diplomat he'd been reading about in the newspapers, becoming instead the serious agent of a hostile foreign Power. Whereupon the Executive would act: the confirmation would oblige it to. It would press the buttons ruthlessly—all of them and hard. Starc would be hunted grimly, not as a missing person now, not even as a murderer, but as the dangerous agent he was.

But that wouldn't happen immediately. He gave himself forty-eight hours at least, knowing his masters mightn't.

It had been dispassionate, trained thinking and it was accident which negated it. The accident's name was Detective Inspector Mellor, and he was a dour and conscientious man. His instructions had been to find a missing diplomat, and his first and most natural call had been at the embassy concerned. The story he had been given there had infuriated him, for he had known at once that it couldn't be all the truth. The embassy had protested total ignorance of motive. They had hinted at a woman but they hadn't known her name. Mellor had suggested some financial difficulty. . . . Yes, that was possible, but it didn't seem likely. Starc was well paid and he lived very quietly. . . . An inquiry at his bank then? But the Inspector would know that that would be most irregular.

Mellor had left the embassy with a suspicion he detested: he was a policeman being asked to make the motions. And his interview with his Superintendent had been far from reassuring. His Superintendent hadn't limited him but he had pointed out that Starc was a diplomatist; he had pointed out too that it was at least a fair assumption that he'd quietly skipped the country. Mellor had hated it. He had a backlog of work and not enough men to cover it. Either they really wanted Starc, in which case they could say so and he'd do his best; or else they didn't, when he could call off his hard-worked men, this scandalous waste of scant resources. The case had offended him—put his professional back up. He had obstinately decided to bring Starc in.

He hadn't any call to be pounding the pavements west of Finsbury Park station in very plain clothes and his private time, but he had arrived in the sleazy jungle of North Four by a process of reasoning which Russell would have approved. Detective Inspector Mellor would have admitted that there had been a good deal of guesswork, but there had been a solid core of logic too. He had been liaisoning with the Executive and, since Starc was a diplomat, he could understand that it seemed well content that Starc should be sought (if he must be sought) as simply a missing person. But there had been a contact with a barmaid too, where Starc had been representing himself as some sort of petty thief. The Executive was handling that side, and Mellor had been too experienced to meddle. But it had made him think. A certain economy was an essential of successful lying, which meant in practice that you told the simplest lie. And the simplest lie about what you were was one which told a part-truth. Why say you were a thief if you didn't know any? Why not a bookmaker, somebody sending messages because his business was illegal? Or why not play it big and hint at drugs? The barmaid, clearly, hadn't been scrupulous. But if you did know a thief, if a thief had put you in mind of thieving, it was possible you'd hole up with just that thief. That was surmise of course, a very thin thread for the academically minded, but this was life and it was the only line Mellor had. Moreover it narrowed the field. London was full of thieves but most of them were English. Starc was a foreigner, an educated man; he wouldn't expect an English thief to credit for long he was really another. Nor would he go to a foreigner, one of his own race especially. But a man who spoke English but wasn't, a man he could impress as something special. . . .

Mellor had decided that it might be a West Indian, but he was much too cautious to be hopeful. He couldn't have sent a subordinate on what most of his mind insisted was a goose-chase: instead he had come in person. He told himself sourly he was getting old; he was playing at detectives. But he didn't quite believe it.

He had taken the tube to Finsbury Park station and had started to walk westwards. He hadn't a map but he was good at streets, and he had just calculated that he wasn't more than a quarter of a mile from his starting-point. He looked around him, profoundly depressed. Three men out of five were black, and all the women. Mellor didn't object to that since he wasn't colour-conscious. What depressed him was the street.

It hadn't been painted in thirty years. There was rubbish in the gutters and a faintly acrid smell. A man passed him on a bicycle, an emery wheel strapped to the handlebars, calling a London Cry which Mellor had imagined had died with the prints which recorded them—Knives and Scissors to grind, ayee-ayee-ayee. There were junk shops and cafés, bursting dustbins on the pavements outside them. He passed a peeling surgery, glancing by habit at the stained brass plate. Dr O'Brien, Dr Kopec, Dr Radhakrishnan. A good policeman, he made a note. A colleague in headquarters would be interested.

He shivered in the gathering dusk, moving his shoulders in his heavy coat. Christ, this was cactus land. And he was looking for a needle in a haystack.

He walked into a café, ordering tea for safety though he detested it, inspecting the cup suspiciously. At the table on one side of him two men were talking in a language he recognized as Polish, and on the other were two West Indians. Across the room was an Indian alone, rather north, Mellor thought, of his countrymen's major beat. He wished the Poles good evening and they politely returned it. He smiled at the West Indians and, after a second's hesitation, they smiled back shyly. They were unshaven and tieless but, by their own magic, clean. Mellor had often noticed it. West Indians weren't fastidious but somehow were always clean: Indians bathed daily, literally religiously, but were people to keep upwind of.

He began to watch the Indian. He was wolfing his food furiously, sausages and the inescapable mashed potatoes. Mellor thought it odd. The Indian had the fine features of the high-caste Hindu. In which case he wouldn't be eating sausages. Or if he were a Mussalman he wouldn't be eating pork. If the sausages were pork. Which reduced it to a Mussalman guzzling beef and liking it. Except that he hadn't the air.

The Indian paid his bill and the two Poles rose with him. They walked to the door and the Indian went out first. The door shut behind him. There was a cry and the unmistakable thump of a heavy calibre pistol.

Stevan Starc hadn't supposed that the best sort of hideout was one furthest from a bus route: on the contrary he had chosen his own for the excellence of its communications, which meant the excellence of the getaway in trouble. His host had a job on British Railways; he wasn't an actual thief but he was the inside man for an experienced gang which looted railway warehouses with contemptuous efficiency. He had accepted Starc for exactly what he had said he was, a jewellery man operating in a very different world but needing, from time to time, the sort of hideaway the police wouldn't promptly look for. He admired Stevan Starc and his money was generous.

The risk wasn't great. It hadn't surprised him when Starc had stained his face brown, for he had explained it convincingly. Starc wasn't trying to pass as an Indian, not amongst other Indians, but he was on to something where, for a vital ten minutes, Europeans must think he was one. Indians rang two immediate bells: one was the abortioners who traded so briskly a mile to the south and the other was maharajahs—jewels.

It was a very good hideout but had one serious disadvantage. Starc was near-starving. He had the delicate stomach of the highly strung man and the cooking defeated him. Rather than offend his hosts he had eaten their food at first, but at once it had griped him. For a day he had been quite ill. Later there had been milk and bread but he couldn't live for long on milk and bread. This evening he was famished. . . . Meat! A steak if he could get it or, if he couldn't, sausages. The cafés in Fonthill Road were as tempting as any restaurant. It was an unnecessary risk though perhaps a small one, but in any case he shouldn't be taking it. He had hesitated, finally succumbed. He checked the stain on his face and hands. His hair was black naturally. Then he went in search of steak.

As it happened he didn't find it, settling instead for sausages. He was ravenous and was eating fast but more than hunger goaded him. He had heard men speaking Polish and for a second his scalp had crawled. He told himself it meant nothing, every language of Europe could be heard within a mile of him, but Poles. . . .

He paid his bill and the Poles rose with him. They walked to the door and he went out first. The door shut behind him. One Pole drew a cosh but Starc threw an arm up. As he fell the other fired.

Detective Inspector Mellor was through the door in four long strides. One of the Poles and the Indian were struggling on the ground, the second Pole standing over them. He had a gun in his hand still, trying to get a second shot in. The Indian was fighting desperately, trying to keep a Pole on top of him. For an instant the other saw a half chance. The gun came up and Mellor kicked it. It spun in a parabola, sliding across the street, banging against the opposite kerb. Inspector Mellor waited. He still knew enough to kick a gun up but he was much too old to mix it. The street was deserted. He said in a small clear voice: 'I'm a police officer.'

The second Pole rose and for a long count of ten both of them stared at him. Finally the second spoke. The language wasn't Polish now. The other shrugged and both men turned. They began to run clumsily, their heavy boots thudding. They swung to the left; were gone.

Mellor turned back to the Indian. He was holding his stomach and fighting for breath.

'Are you wounded?'

'He missed.'

Mellor put his hand out and the Indian took it in his left. His shirt had been torn and for a moment it fell open. His chest was as white as Mellor's.

The white-chested Indian said weakly: 'Give me your other hand' and, as Mellor bent down, he took it. He bunched his knees suddenly, jamming his feet in Mellor's stomach. Then he pulled as he straightened his legs. Mellor went over helplessly. It was a sacrifice throw but for a man already lying it was perfect. Mellor, as he swung over, swore. He was certainly getting old to fall for that one. He remembered to tuck his head in but he landed very heavily. He was a man of middle age and he was shaken. He lay for a moment, collecting himself. The two West Indians had come out of the café and were watching him impassively, for this wasn't a part of London where you intruded on private fighting. Mellor picked himself up, recovering the pistol. He looked both ways but Starc had gone.

Forty minutes later he was in his Superintendent's room. On the table was a clutter of photographs, maps and a pistol. The Superintendent was recapitulating: 'You're sure it was Starc?'

'I am. I couldn't swear it in court because I didn't spot him when he looked like an Indian. You know what a lawyer could make of that.'

'I'm not a lawyer. And his speech?'

'Not an Indian's English. Nor an Englishman's either.'

'And these other two men?'

'They were talking Polish. I picked up a little Polish in the war.'

'But they changed to something else?'

'Positively not Polish.'

The Superintendent nodded at the pistol. 'That isn't Polish either.' He thought for some time, then picked up a telephone. He spoke briefly but listened much. When he hung up again he reached for a map, putting a pin in the heart of North Four. 'That's where it happened?'

'Yes.'

The Superintendent looked at the scale of the map then, with a blunt blue pencil, drew a quarter-mile circle round the pin. 'I want that beaten house to house.'

'It might take a week.'

'It might but I hope it doesn't. What we were looking for was a missing diplomat, now we're looking for a diplomat whom somebody's trying to kill.' The Superintendent smiled a policeman's smile. 'That rather changes—well, the politics.'

'I take the point.'

'Moreover the men after him were Poles. Poles who could

speak another language. Poles who were carrying a firearm made a long way east of Warsaw.'

'I see that too.'

'Then take all the men you want. I've full authority to turn the heat on.' The Superintendent looked at the map again and his mouth shut grimly. 'Authority,' he said, 'and orders too.' He pointed at the circle with the blunt blue pencil. 'Comb it and comb it well. Find him—we've got to.'

CHAPTER 9

Alex Gorjan had been at Nags Cottage only part of a day and one night, but already he had settled to a routine which he had decided would amuse him. Nags Cottage was itself diverting, since it wasn't a cottage at all but a substantial house. There were six bedrooms and, incredibly, six bathrooms too. Gorjan knew this because he had slipped away to count them. He had heard that the airier sort of psychiatrist had elaborate explanations about the compulsion to over-cleanliness: Gorjan himself thought it wasteful—anti-social. He took a bath when he felt he needed one or when the relaxation of hot water tempted him. Six bathrooms were simply wicked.

But the so-called cottage was undeniably comfortable. There were an Italian cook and her cousin as housemaid, a jobbing gardener from the village nearby, and a handyman-car-washer who lived in separate quarters. Since the house was called a cottage his cottage was called a lodge. The food was good and the wine, if undistinguished, potable, and there were pleasant views across a golf course which considered itself exclusive. Gorjan had realized that Nags Cottage was a bastard sham. Few Englishmen could live like this and he suspected fewer wished to. But the atmosphere was English-plus right down to the careful reticences. Nikola Mitrovic had hinted that there might be certain annoyances; Mellion Lee might be boring about his country's too easy wealth; he might even make vague suggestions which, if ever reduced to paper, would be formally improper. But so far he had done neither. At dinner, which had been excellent, he had been the accomplished and worldly host. He had let Gorjan do the talking, sliding in an occasional question, extremely well informed, even, when they had skirted science, surprisingly well informed. And it hadn't been disappointing to discover that Lee and Margaret Palfrey shared a bedroom. Alexander Gorjan had shrugged. He'd been mewed up in hospital and she'd thrown herself at him. He could live without an encore and he settled to enjoy himself. This house was an absurdity, its capitalist roots a scandal. But a man could be content here.

Mellion Lee seemed happy too—Margaret Palfrey had noticed it. Observation was an essential of both her professions, and she wasn't insensitive to the moods of the men around her. There was something new with Mellion Lee, though she couldn't quite pin it. Normally he drank a bit, nothing outrageous, but in the evening he would take a few. And he ate very little. But now he had reversed it, drinking almost nothing but eating with appetite. She had heard that other voice again, his father's voice, dropping assured crisp orders to the handyman. And he hadn't been taking sleeping pills. Last night he had woken, pulling her towards him, not thinking of his technique now, the books he considered bible, but taking her almost attritively. He'd enjoyed himself greatly and for the first time she'd enjoyed him.

And he'd surprised her more than physically. There had been sardonic comments about the diplomatic world which she would never have believed if she hadn't heard them, and his manner with Gorjan had astonished her. She had expected a ragged compromise, deference struggling with a native but never to be admitted mediocrity, but no, he had treated him with the easy respect of equals. And though he mightn't know much science he had known very well how to talk to a scientist.

In the enormous bed next morning Margaret sighed. She was a woman still, though there had been men who had rudely denied it, and Mellion Lee was beginning to interest her. The unexpectedness changed sigh to a tiny gasp. Under the diplomat, the rich American, was something called Mellion Lee. A vigorous something and almost happy; and Margaret believed she knew the reason. The Mellion Lees weren't happy because the breaks came in: all their well-ordered lives the luck had run their way, or if it hadn't they could always go out and buy it. So this wouldn't be material, some sudden promotion or office coup. No, Mellion Lee had faced something, Mellion had decided. She didn't know what and she didn't care.

She rolled from the bed and dressed, brushing her hair carefully. For a woman of forty—well, forty-one—she thought it was rather nice. She went downstairs to the dining-room. Lee had gone out with Gorjan, showing him the Bentley. There were coffee and milk on hot-plates and a basket of rolls. She didn't eat breakfast and the Italian servants knew it. She rang the bell and, when the maid appeared, said firmly: 'Eggs and bacon. Lots of it.'

James Scobell and Russell were talking in the solid but unpompous comfort of Russell's room at the Security Executive. Scobell was rubbing his carefully shaved jowl, saying a little doubtfully: 'It's a much smaller party at Nags Cottage than I expected. Just Mellion Lee, that woman of his, and Alex Gorjan himself.'

'From which you deduce?'

'I don't deduce. I simply point out that what we were both assuming was that Lee would try to *tempt* Gorjan. He'd boost the American way of life which all intelligent Europeans know perfectly well means the American standard of living. For that I should have expected more than one American. A principal, in fact, but chorus too.'

'No doubt. But we also agreed that Lee would fail. Whereafter he might try something else, some variety of pressure, possibly blackmail. That would be amateur too, and that might fail disastrously. People like you and me would be left to sweep the bits up.'

'We should. So we made an alliance expressly to avoid it if we could. But I'm not quite sure what you're getting at.'

Russell poured sherry and Scobell drank half of his. Charles Russell suppressed a flinch but didn't comment. Across his own glass he said: 'To sell the American way of life you'd use more than one American. But for any sort of skulduggery, even the most maladroit, the fewer in the ploy the better.'

'I hadn't thought of that side.' James Scobell was reflective.

'Oh, I wouldn't call it thinking—just a springboard for thought.'

'But it does fit the facts, though I agree only negatively. The implication, if I may use the word, is that there won't be any sales talk. They'll go straight to the pressure. God knows what sort of it. That's where we're hamstrung. You think this Margeret Palfrey's in it too?'

'I simply don't know.'

There was a silence while both men thought. They had exchanged their papers, the Executive's file on Margaret against James Scobell's on Lee. It had made Russell think—what he would have agreed was really thinking. He remembered that he had described Lee to Palliser as a tall man in English clothes, an American who had lived in Europe rather too long. It wasn't a description which he wished to withdraw but now he would have wanted to expand it. For the Lees had a history—tough, extrovert and successful. Mellion Lee might look like the stereotype of a middle-piece diplomatist but whether he liked it or not his blood was a great deal thicker. Russell wasn't a geneticist but he had read about genes. Mellion Lee would have some odd ones. There had been that killing in the great rush west where the Lees hadn't struck it lucky, then, half a generation later, the astonishing affair of the railroad franchise. That had meant money and they'd held it through the bad years, plenty to launch Mellion's father into the newspaper jungle. From which he'd emerged with a score of scalps, a wholly ruthless winner.

. . . Quite a family for a diplomat.

James Scobell broke the silence. 'Then what do we do now?'

'I don't think there's much we can. For one thing we may be entirely wrong and for another we've got our hands tied.'

'While a diplomat makes a mess of it? Till we have to go in with the brooms?'

'I'm afraid that's what we started from.'

'You've told Copeman of this? You've warned him?'

'I wouldn't say warned him.' Russell was dry but still urbane; he added meticulously: 'Oliver Copeman has very precise instructions.'

'Which cover some foolish action by an amateur like Lee?'

'No,' Russell said, 'I couldn't swear that.'

Oliver Copeman had indeed had very precise instructions, though they hadn't included breaking Mellion Lee's safe. By the standards of the Executive he wasn't an expert locksmith, but he was a man of varied competence and the safe at Nags Cottage had been an intolerable temptation. Nobody, he had decided, had the right to have a safe like that, an antiquated box of ancient steel with a lock which a genuine expert could have opened in thirty seconds. Copeman himself would take a little longer, but he needn't burn and he needn't use explosives —just a straightforward job in the small hours to relieve the monotony. For Oliver Copeman was bored. Alexander Gorjan had arrived for tea on Thursday, whereafter nothing had happened whatever. On Friday morning Lee had taken him driving in the Bentley, then there had been lunch, an ample one Copeman had gathered, and Gorjan had gone to bed to sleep it off. Afterwards dinner and a good deal of chatter later. Mrs Palfrey had gone up early but the men had sat talking till well past midnight. It seemed about as innocent as anything could be, and it was Copeman's impression that he was wasting his time. It wasn't an occupation he was used to.

It was now three o'clock on the morning of the Saturday and Copeman with a small black bag was in the room they called the library. He had made his reconnaissance the night before and he hadn't considered failure; he had given himself ten minutes and in practice he took nine. The door of the safe swung open.

Copeman examined the contents methodically. He hadn't let himself speculate on what he might find and in fact he found little. There was a pile of notes and he counted them quickly, flipping them through his lightly gloved fingers. . . . Three thousand dollars—far too much to keep around even if the safe had been a good one. How the rich asked for it! And there was a single file of papers in an unmarked cover. Copeman put the money back, opening the file.

At once he was interested. There were perhaps sixty pages, divided into unequal parts by cardboard separators. The first section was diagrams, graphs and what Copeman took to be the prints of complicated electrical circuits. All were clearly numbered. The second part meant nothing, twenty pages of algebraic symbols tantalisingly salted with an occasional calculation in straight arithmetic. Each group of symbols, each calculation, was again carefully numbered. Copeman looked a second time. He wasn't a mathematician but he could recognize an equation.

He turned to the third part, his eyebrows rising. This was the largest section and it was words. It was laid out as *Question* and *Comment on Answer*. Copeman read Question 24 and shrugged. The question was framed to be answered yes or no but he didn't understand it. He went on to the Comment:

Comment on Answer

(a) If answer is positive, refer subject to Diagram 17. A squared area has been blocked in in blue pencil where the abscissa meets the ordinate. Ask whether the relationship remains purely linear.

(b) If answer is negative, refer subject back to Equation 36. In the light of the negative answer can it still be said that Theta remains a function. . . ?

Copeman pursed his lips in a silent whistle. He shut the safe but didn't lock it, the file in his hand still. Then he sat down to think. This must go to London, to the photocopy boys and fast. And it wouldn't be so easy.

It wouldn't be so easy because he'd have to take a car. Copeman looked at his watch. It was three-twenty precisely and to London on empty roads perhaps forty minutes. Then it would be up to the Executive, but if they could work fast enough there was a reasonable chance that he could manage to put the file back before the maids woke at six. That was a working risk, but taking a car was a very poor bet indeed. The garages weren't by the lodge but built on to the house at right angles. Moreover the maids lived above them. Still, the drive sloped sharply downwards so he needn't start the engine and wake the women. He could coast away almost silently but returning he'd be stuck.

Copeman decided coolly that the car didn't matter. Provided he put the papers back it wouldn't be important that a handyman was sacked. Colonel Russell would replace him. So he'd motor back from London but he'd leave the car down at the lodge. Then up to the house on foot, back to the vital safe. When the house woke they'd miss the car, and promptly they'd dismiss him. He might plead he'd a girl in London.

His excuse wouldn't matter once the file was safely back

again. That file was as hot as hell.

Oliver Copeman went out to the garage silently. He had the key on a ring and he opened the sliding doors. It took him some time since he did it very carefully, then he stood for a moment thinking. There were the Bentley and an American convertible—a cow of a car, he thought her, for she rolled abominably. In traffic the Bentley could beat her, but in the middle of the night on empty roads she could show hairy heels to a middle-aged Bentley. Copeman edged her out cautiously, then, when the preposterous thing was rolling, opened the door. As she slid down the drive he checked the petrol. Yes. . . .

Once past the lodge he started the engine. Five litres, he guessed, and maybe more. He'd use every one of them.

Thirty-five minutes later he was at the Security Executive. He went straight to the duty officer, tossing the file on his desk.

'That's just about as hot as it can be.'

The duty officer flicked the pages. 'It does look pretty sinister. All that mathematics. . . . Where did you steal it?'

'I didn't steal—I borrowed. That's the point. I've got to put it back before the house wakes. How long to photocopy?'

'There's nobody in Photography in the middle of the night.'

'Could we do it ourselves?'

'Probably. Very badly.'

'I know a bit and there's a good machine. We'll have to try.'

When they had finished Copeman looked at his watch again. They had taken just over the hour. 'I'll just about make it.'

The duty officer nodded at the photocopy. 'And this lot?' he asked.

'They're to be in Colonel Russell's hands the minute he wakes. Serve them with his morning tea.'

'On your orders but not otherwise. He hates working outside the office. If they're not really as hot as you think they are you're for it.'

Copeman said dourly: 'I'll take the risk.'

Colonel Russell was still in a dressing-gown as Lord Normer shut the file of photocopies. Normer asked reflectively: 'Now where did you find this?'

'I'll tell you that later when you've told me what it is.'

'It's a questionnaire, a brief. And it's a very good brief indeed.'

'Could a diplomat have done it?'

'None that I've met or ever expect to.'

'Then it was done *for* a diplomat. The original of that file was found in a safe belonging to a man called Mellion Lee. Who is Scientific Counsellor at the American Embassy. In whose house, at this moment, Alex Gorjan is staying.'

Lord Normer said: 'God in heaven.'

'Yes. . . . Now tell me about that questionnaire.'

'It's been done by a first-class scientist but it's been done to be used by an intelligent layman. If the layman knows some mathematics so much the better. It puzzled me when I read it first. These questions could only be answered by a second scientist, so why should the first take the trouble to reduce highly technical material to a more or less Yes–No form to be administered by a non-scientist? Why not go straight to the other scientist who talks the same language you do? And of course get a better answer. As I told you, that puzzled me at first. Now I'm afraid it doesn't.'

'You're beginning to frighten me.' Russell rose unexpectedly, striding to the wall and back. Opposite Normer he smiled almost shyly. 'There's something I'd like to ask you but the possible answer scares me.'

'All right, let me help you.' Lord Normer lit a deliberate pipe and Russell sat down slowly. 'I think you were going to ask me where those questions would lead if answered.'

'I was trying to face that one—yes.'

'I may assume that it was Alex Gorjan to whom they were going to be put?'

Charles Russell nodded.

'Then if they had been put to Gorjan by an intelligent man who had had the chance to discuss this questionnaire with the scientist who framed it, a great deal would have been learnt about Gorjan's work. I don't put it higher since I don't think I need. Not his secret—we agreed before that he didn't have one—but this brief was drawn up by a scientist who had been making much the same guesses I have about what Gorjan's close to.' Lord Normer considered, then went on still more carefully. 'Put it like this. If I had the answers to those questions I'd be right on Gorjan's tail. I might not reach what he would since I'm clever enough to know he's cleverer. But I'd be running down the same straight road. And so, I must tell you, would half a dozen others.' Lord Normer tapped the photocopies. 'Including the American I'm sure did this. I'd guess it was Harry Leibnitz.'

Russell murmured an apology, walking to the telephone. When he had his number he said briefly: 'Mortimer? Get in touch with Copeman at Mellion Lee's house in Surrey. Copeman lives at the lodge and there isn't a separate telephone. Take your own car or mine. Don't be seen contacting him unless you have to, but get him to ring me back. If it seems really urgent *bring* him back. That would blow him of course, but it may be unavoidable. You've full discretion within the limits that I must speak to him by noon.'

Russell put the receiver back, returning to Lord Normer. His housekeeper had brought coffee and Russell poured it. Lord

Normer said: 'There's one thing that still puzzles me.'

'Just one?'

Normer ignored it. 'We've been assuming that these questions would be put to Alex Gorjan?'

'We have.'

'But why should he answer them?'

Charles Russell's face was suddenly a stone. 'That,' he said grimly, 'I mean to find out.'

CHAPTER 10

When Normer had gone Charles Russell finished dressing and walked to the Executive. He had an appointment with Nikola Mitrovic at ten o'clock and it was one he had been looking forward to. Nikola Mitrovic was always worth attention, for his appointment had been in what Russell considered the classic tradition of choosing a country's representatives abroad, namely that you picked as typical a specimen as was available of the ruling junta of your nation. Nikola had detractors, the diplomats *de carrière* of more sophisticated states, and in the artificially isolated world of professional diplomacy he was apt to be dismissed as simply a promoted brigand. Russell thought the judgement dangerously superficial—dangerous to those who made it. In any case he much preferred to deal with Nikola Mitrovic than with men who were civil servants with pretensions, and, as he walked briskly to the Executive, he was wondering whether foreigners thought the same. . . . Her Majesty's ambassadors—how did foreigners really see them? Their Excellencies took instructions from a Minister with a sesquipedalian style and title. In form, that is. In fact they were at the beck and call of some faceless committee they had probably never heard of. Which of course was the ruling junta, which of course was in that sense right. And foreigners weren't fools; foreigners would scent the shams at once. Beneath the formal hand-kissing, the automatic knighthood, was an errand-boy in fancy dress.

Charles Russell smiled. They kissed hands in the Confederacy but only a pretty woman's, and rule by committee wasn't yet universal. So he was walking to an appointment which he expected to be fruitful. Nikky wouldn't be wasting his time.

At ten o'clock, politely punctual, Nikola Mitrovic was shown in. Russell noticed that he had lost a little weight. He was evidently worried but his manner hadn't changed. As he sat down he said: 'I've come to propose a deal.'

'That's one of the things I'm here for.'

'Let's start at Starc and move from there. Starc, as you

know, has bolted and the police are trying to find him. I've also good reason to suppose you're not.'

'May I ask what good reason?'

'Simply that if you had been you'd have found him.'

'Well. . . .'

Nikola Mitrovic waved a hand. 'It isn't important. What is important is that last time I came to see you I didn't tell you everything I knew. I'd had a tip-off that Starc was working for what I then called the other side, the other kind of communist and their enormously powerful ally. Our enemies, in fact—why we sent Alex Gorjan here. And what you told *me* was that within hours of his arrival here an attempt had been made on his life. Hours after that again Starc disappeared, after beating up Petar, whom you'll probably have guessed I'd ordered to tail him. I didn't much like doing it but I'd nobody better. Petar hasn't told the police but he naturally told me.'

'We'd guessed most of this but I'm grateful to know it.'

'What else have you guessed?'

Russell said blandly: 'Plenty,' and Mitrovic grinned.

'Yes, I know I'm on lead. So my own guess is that Starc and the attempt on Gorjan were very much connected.'

'They were—we've just confirmed it. We still hold the two failed-murderers, and they've admitted that their orders came from Starc. We could have broken them sooner but we've English inhibitions. Not that we can ever use their statements. So unless Petar talks, and I take it you won't let him, there'll be no charge against Starc, big or small.' Charles Russell leant forward. 'Do you *want* him charged?'

'I do not.'

'Do you even want him found?'

Nikola Mitrovic shrugged. 'I was really rather hoping he'd be out of the country.'

'Alas, he is not.' Colonel Russell was suddenly formal. 'Starc has been seen in North London disguised as an Indian. And two men were with him. They were apparently Poles but they also spoke the language of what you last referred to as your enormously powerful enemy. They were carrying a gun which had been made in that country and they were trying to kill Stevan Starc.'

There was a formidable silence which Mitrovic broke at last. He had finished his thinking and his matter-of-fact voice showed it. 'The penalty of failure—yes? Or was it simply to shut Starc's mouth?'

'Perhaps it was both.'

'The police will find Starc?'

'Yes, if I know my police. I'm perfectly happy to concede them the first shot at him.'

'And after they find him?'

'That rather depends on you. Assume they don't also find

those Poles. If they did it would be awkward, since Starc would be essential as a witness. But let's assume they don't, or not at once. So what they do find is still a missing diplomat. There'll be no charge against Starc, but in the very strange circumstances the police would almost certainly consult me. What would you want us to do?'

'Simply a missing diplomat? A nervous breakdown perhaps?' Mitrovic sounded happier.

'I'd leave all the lying to you.'

'Accepted.' His Excellency was unoffended. 'So you'd quietly hand him back to me?'

'That's how I see it now. Personal delivery at your embassy's front door. After all he's still a diplomat.'

'You're a very good friend.'

Russell said urbanely: 'But I'm also an official and officials want a quid pro quo.'

'What's the quid?'

'I've two men of your nationality whom I'm holding quite illegally. Naturally I had plans for their disposal but if you'd care to help me I could make things a good deal simpler.'

'Done.' Mitrovic hadn't hesitated. 'There's a ship of my flag in the Port of London now. She was due to sail tomorrow but I can make it immediately. I'll phone you her name and I'll speak to the captain. Have your men there at the time I tell you.' Mitrovic smiled a gritty smile. 'I'll be pleased to take them off you, very pleased.'

He would, he thought—he'd be wholly delighted. He'd put up a black and this might expunge it. Starc would have been a valuable lead domestically. He'd bungled it and lost him but now he had a chance again. Meanwhile he had two others on account. This was his lucky day. He said again happily: 'Send them straight to my ship.'

Russell looked at his watch. It was early yet for alcohol but this was an occasion for a judicious drink. He went to his cupboard, pouring sherry for himself and slivovich for the ambassador. He had bought it specially for him, since he knew he didn't like sherry and Russell hated to see it wasted on a spirit-drinker's palate. With a remembered gesture Mitrovic tossed off his slivovich and Russell sipped his wine. Presently he asked thoughtfully: 'And the original deal you were talking about?'

'Ah, we rather got off that one.' Mitrovic was relaxed again. Russell poured another slivovich and His Excellency repeated the ritual gulp. When the dubious brew was working he went on: 'I still want to keep Gorjan in England.'

'Nikky, I beg you, *think*. I can hold two of your countrymen illegally but only because their entry itself was so illegal that nobody knows they're here. Nobody but Starc, that is. But if you think I can hold a reputable scientist whose name is in

all the papers, who's known to have been in hospital . . .'
Russell looked up in quick inquiry. 'If you want him to stay
here, why don't you tell him to?'

'You misunderstand me. I shall.'

'Then why ask me to keep him?'

But Mitrovic wasn't embarrassed. 'I admit it's a little tricky.
Things in my country are as difficult as they've ever been—
my latest information is that they've never been more critical.
So we can't send Gorjan back there, but if he's well enough
to be allowed out of hospital temporarily on a visit which,
by the way, I authorized reluctantly, the chances are that he'll
be finally discharged quite soon. It's going to look odd if he's
left to kick his heels here, and we don't like things looking
odd. Your newspapers aren't fools.'

'I quite see that but I simply can't hide him.' Charles Russell was conveying an irrevocable decision.

'I wasn't quite asking you to hide him.'

'Then what?'

Mitrovic said deliberately: 'I want you to find him a job.'

'You once said he'd never work for us.'

'He would if he were told to.'

There was another long silence while this time Russell
thought. He asked at last and he sounded incredulous: 'You
mean you'd let us use him?'

'I would—*we* would. And in case you should think that it's
only that old fool Mitrovic I can show you my instructions if
you insist. And, come to think of it, they aren't so extraordinary. We don't want Gorjan killed by one side, nor attempts
to seduce him by the other. Not that we think they've the
least chance of doing it but we properly resent their trying.
That's what's really behind this visit to Mellion Lee's, and
the whole thing's very dangerous for a man as sick as Alex.
I didn't want to let him go but I dare say you can guess
that I was made to. And, perhaps, why.'

'I can guess,' Russell said. 'I can see they could bring pressure.'

'They have and we didn't like it, but their money's very
welcome. Still, we can't have Gorjan hounded. So what we
need now is a kind of protection—cover. Yours. And we'll pay
for it too.'

'By letting Gorjan work for us?'

'It'll be a matter for negotiation, naturally. The proposition
I'm authorized to make you is that you can employ Gorjan on
any matter you wish but one. That will need definition but it
shouldn't be insuperable. You know his reputation and I'm offering you eighty per cent of him. That ought to be worth while to
you and it's well worth while to us. Once he's openly your man,
a direct English interest, we can think about the future. That
is, if my country has one. And if it doesn't, if we go under——'

'You talked about cover so what's the story?'

'Alex will ask you for political asylum. It's happened before, it'll satisfy the newspapers, and you can stick the moulting feather in your public English hats. Gorjan will have defected —East to West. Of course it won't be true, but you left all the lying to me.'

Russell laughed. 'That makes us all square.' He reflected again. 'You seem to be trusting us.'

'Oddly enough we are. You're a deceptively tough people and crooked as they come. You're so crooked that the only way to hold you is a gentleman's agreement.'

Charles Russell bowed, then returned to his sherry; he said at length: 'I'll have to talk to my Minister. It's tempting, though. So as soon as Gorjan leaves Mellion Lee's. . . .'

A telephone on his desk rang sharply and Russell frowned. But it must be important or they wouldn't be interrupting him. He apologized to Mitrovic, picking the receiver up. His secretary was saying anxiously: 'I'm sorry to break in, sir, but there's a message from Major Mortimer. He says it's pretty urgent.'

'Please put him through.'

Russell listened intently, his lean face hardening. 'Very well,' he said finally. 'Come back to London and bring Copeman with you. Bring him straight here and report to me personally.' He put down the telephone. Mitrovic had risen but Russell waved him down again. With a scrupulous under-emphasis he said: 'Alex Gorjan has disappeared.'

CHAPTER 11

Mellion Lee had never intended to sell the American way of life to Alex Gorjan, far less to persuade him to live in the United States. He had remembered that the very important visitor to London, his father's friend and contemporary, had spoken of persuasion, adding in a manner which he had imagined to be meaningful but which in fact had struck Lee as inanely cloak and dagger that there was more than one sort of persuasion. Mellion Lee smiled ironically. What had the fool been thinking of—granted, that is, that he had been capable of thinking? A crazy kidnapping, a light aircraft from Black-bushe, then the landing in a meadow somewhere in Wales, the waiting saloon (of course it would be black) with the petrol in jerrycans for the next leg on to Ireland. Finally to Shannon, quiet and almost provincial since the big jets could overfly it. There something would be standing by. . . .

Such a plan was a pipe dream.

And so was the other, even the possibility that Gorjan could be tempted by money or what money bought. Lee had been doing some simple research on Alexander Gorjan and it had convinced him very quickly that the suggestion wasn't a starter. Gorjan was a communist and proud of his race and nation. His tastes, though expensive, weren't tainted by ambition, and his country could meet them generously. Moreover it did so. The bland assumption that every man had his price was at least more realistic than an old man's hints at an unspecified skulduggery, but applied to Gorjan it wasn't less impractical. That approach would be unfruitful too.

Mellion Lee had always had another. It appealed to him intellectually since he started with an advantage. He wasn't a physicist, he knew nothing of microwaves, but he knew that the great division wasn't between one sort of scientist and another but between men with a scientific discipline and those without it. His own skills were somewhat rusty but his training, the way he thought, remained. He would have a language in common with Alex Gorjan, above all he could ask him questions which a scientist would understand. He certainly couldn't frame them, and far less assess the answers, but he was confident he could handle it. Lee had never believed that Gorjan had a simple secret: to a man of his training the word itself was suspect, and he would have agreed with Lord Normer that if Gorjan had possessed what was popularly called a secret he would never have been allowed to leave his country. But he did have a line and he was running it brilliantly. That was common knowledge. He had experience, maybe know-how.

Mellion Lee meant to get it.

There had been a series of enormously expensive telephone calls across the Atlantic and, as their result, a file had been flown over and delivered to Lee personally. He had studied it thoroughly, telephoning again on passages which had puzzled him, briefing himself carefully within what he realized were the limits of his competence. He had a great stake to play for and he could put his motive simply. The word wasn't one which you often heard in embassies, and in the circles which Lee patronized off duty it would raise an embarrassed snigger. The word was patriotism. Mellion Lee was an American; he wished passionately to serve. Usefully, he thought, for once. The wasted years, the sterile talk and protocol. . . . And his father was ashamed of him, a diplomat, suspect of futility and of English affectations, half a man. But this was opportunity and he a Lee. His father might be ashamed of him but he wasn't ashamed of his father. A tyrant, yes, and by some judgements wicked. That wasn't really relevant: his good opinion mattered still. It mattered very much.

Lee had planned carefully to earn it, deciding he wouldn't

rush things. Gorjan's visit to Nags Cottage had been arranged from tea-time on Thursday till Monday evening, so Lee wouldn't be pressed for time. He'd give Gorjan Thursday, all of Friday, to relax in; he'd build up the atmosphere, friendly and neutral; he'd lower the defences, particularly the unconscious ones. Then he'd start work on Saturday.

Mellion Lee had planned that too. He'd had a brief from America but he'd also had something more. It was a leather case, six inches by four and perhaps an inch deep. Mellion Lee had opened it, shutting it quickly, suppressing what had almost been a shiver. That part would be for Margaret. Margaret Palfrey had once been a doctor. That was why she was at Nags Cottage.

He woke at five on Saturday morning, conscious that he wouldn't sleep again. He looked at Margaret Palfrey but decided quite coolly against her. He was forty-five and he had work to do. Instead he slipped from the warm bed quietly, putting on a dressing-gown. He might as well use the extra hours, there was a point which still slightly worried him, and it was extraordinary how the disciplines of youth came back at you. He *must* get it right; he'd even telephone if necessary. Leibnitz wouldn't relish being woken just as he had gone to bed, but Leibnitz would have to take it.

Mellion Lee went downstairs to the library. He switched on the light and walked to the safe; he put his hand on the handle and at once the door moved. . . . So he'd been unpardonably careless, he must really watch the little things. He pulled the door open, frowning, and looked in. The file had gone.

He sat down, shocked but calm, to think it over. The money was there still, so it couldn't have been a burglar: a burglar would have stolen the money and left the file. Instead they had picked the file.

Somebody had been watching him, somebody somehow knew. He'd lost before he started.

Mellion Lee looked at his watch. It was ten-past five and faintly lightening. He couldn't go back to bed again and there was nothing he could do. He went upstairs, shaving and dressing quickly. He might as well go for a walk—a walk might steady him. As he unlatched the elaborate front door he saw that the garage was open.

It was a moment before the penny dropped. The handyman had the second key and the handyman could drive. The convertible wasn't there. And nor was the file.

Lee began to chew on it. Assume this odd-job man was some sort of agent. Then he wouldn't be quite a fool; he would realize that simply stealing a file wouldn't be very clever. For one thing there could easily be a duplicate, and for another Lee himself would be bound to miss it some time. Whereupon he could change his plan, and the agent's employers would be groping in the dark again. But copy it, slip it back, interpret it at your leisure. . . .

Mellion Lee let his breath out in a long soft sigh. That was the intention—he'd have done the same himself. So the handyman meant to come back. He'd plan to return the file and lock the safe. The car would be missed since he'd hardly dare drive back in it in daylight, but he'd have a story about the car and for that he'd take his medicine. It wouldn't affect an achieved success. The file would be back and its owner wholly ignorant. And they'd plant another agent when in outrage he sacked this one.

Mellion Lee walked down to the lodge. It was empty, as he'd expected. The door was unlocked and he began to search perfunctorily. The handyman must return before the maids stirred so he hadn't much time for searching. Still, it was worth a confirmation if there was one. But Lee could find nothing—no weapon, no papers, not even the *Times* or *Telegraph* obliquely to hint that this servant wasn't quite what he said he was. Lee wasn't disappointed for he had found what he really wished to. It was a serviceable coil of clothes line and a short brass poker. He looked at his watch again. It was five forty-two and the maids woke at six.

. . . He's running it pretty fine.

Lee slipped behind the open door as a car stopped outside. He heard its door shut quietly. All the odds were that the handyman would go first to the house, but Lee braced himself instinctively. Nobody came near the lodge. He heard the faint shuffle of rubber-soled shoes, then silence as it died away.

It was five fifty-three when he heard it again. He had put down the rope but he still held the poker. It was a stout little poker and beautifully balanced. And that, Lee thought, was just as well. This wasn't his trade. He'd have just one chance and he couldn't afford to miss it.

A man came by him, hatless, and Lee struck. Oliver Copeman reeled and for a second Lee felt sick. Then Copeman fell finally.

Mellion Lee put down the poker. Copeman was on his face. There was a considerable contusion, swelling as Lee looked at it, but no blood at all. He was grateful for that. He dragged Copeman to his bed and somehow got him on to it—legs first, then the rest of him. He seemed monstrously heavy. Mellion Lee collected the rope, tying Copeman to the bed and stepping back. It looked anything but a professional job but it should hold a stunned man for an hour. And that was all he wanted. An hour to get to London in the Bentley—himself, Gorjan and Margaret.

He walked from the lodge, lighting a cigarette. It was the

first since he had been there for he had noticed that the handyman didn't smoke. Mellion Lee began to smile. He had just stunned a servant and had bound him to his bed; he was a Counsellor of Embassy. Now his smile was a laugh, astonished but almost gay. He had forty-five years and he'd never been less aware of them. The cigarette tasted wonderful. He had forgotten his spectacles but he didn't seem to need them. So this was the world in this clear cool dawn. His senses were extraordinarily acute. From the house he heard the tinkle of an alarm clock. That would be the maids', of course. Six o'clock precisely.

He'd been a good one, that handyman.

Mellion Lee walked back to the house and straight into the bedroom. Margaret Palfrey was awake but she wasn't yet dressing. He said to her precisely: 'Please get up quickly. We're going to London.'

'What's happened?'

'I'll tell you that later.'

She looked at him but didn't answer. There was an authority about him now, and even a certain ease: he'd moved further than decision. That had been taken and it had noticeably changed him. Now he had changed again. Mr Mellion Lee was a Lee in action.

Margaret dressed and began to pack a bag.

'You won't have time for that.'

'I——'

'Please come with me.'

She followed him silently to Gorjan's room. Gorjan was sleeping and Mellion Lee woke him. He repeated the formula, the same tone of quiet authority.

'Please get up quickly. We're going back to London.'

Gorjan sat up slowly and Margaret Palfrey watched him. His face was expressionless but it was clear he was thinking. He was surprised but he didn't seem frightened. He was reviewing the possibilities and it was evident he liked none of them. Presently he said sharply: 'Why?'

'I'll explain in the car.'

'I'd rather hear now.'

'There isn't time.'

There were ten seconds' silence as Gorjan thought again. He said at length mildly: 'All right,' swinging his legs from the bed. When he was standing he turned towards the wardrobe. He swung again suddenly, quick as a cat, rushing Mellion Lee in an animal's compact charge.

Thirty years earlier, in an expensive New England prep., Mellion Lee had taken boxing lessons. Now he raced instinctively; he put up his right arm and poked out his left. It would have earned an approving murmur at the A.B.A. but it didn't stop Gorjan. He blinked as the gentlemanly left caught him somewhere below the eye but it didn't even slow him. He came in savagely, bent almost double now, hooking with both hands, wickedly low. He was a couple of inches higher than the target he'd been aiming for, but he hit Lee squarely and a foot below the belt. Mellion Lee folded and his head came down. Gorjan swung his knee up. He was a couple of inches out again but he pulped Lee's nose. Lee staggered back, falling across a chair.

He was up again astonishingly fast, his face a bloody mask. He was holding the chair and for a second Gorjan hesitated.

So did Margaret Palfrey. She had never seen men fighting in her life. Boxing was anathema, her friends disapproved of it, and free-style brawling wasn't something which often happened in the snootier literary journalism. What did a woman do? There was a literature where she did plenty: she helped her man. Margaret knew for she'd once tried her hand at it. For the money of course, and under a pseudonym. It had looked very easy but she had found that it was not. As Ursula Urquhart no publisher would look at her. She had thought it extremely unfair. Why, she could write those other women under the table.

Ursula Urquhart had remained unpublished.

She stood undecided. The second of suspense had gone. Gorjan was coming in again and Lee had the chair still. He raised it and swung, and Gorjan dived under it. The chair went across the bedroom, smashing the wardrobe's mirror. Both men went down. Gorjan was on top and he was very much the stronger. He was strangling Lee efficiently, his thumbs on his throat, not pressing the windpipe directly but one on each side of it, inwards. Two terrified maids were standing in the doorway. Mellion Lee was weakening.

Suddenly it was over and it was Lee who was standing. He staggered and Margaret ran to him. He pushed her away, pointing at Alex Gorjan. He was lying on his back and he was motionless. Lee said thickly through his bloody mask: 'Look him over.'

Margaret Palfrey knelt down. She felt Gorjan's pulse and she raised an eyelid. 'He's unconscious,' she said.

'Hell, I can see it.' Lee was choking still and furious.

'Did you manage to hit him?'

'Not where it would knock him out.'

'Then I think he's had some sort of stroke. I'd better ring a doctor, I——'

'No.' Mellion Lee had knelt down in turn, but facing away from Gorjan. Feeling behind him he worked the limp left arm across his shoulder, holding the hand with his own. His right arm groped for Gorjan's crutch, sliding at last between it. Lee lifted him in a clumsy fireman's carry. He staggered again and almost fell, but finally he steadied. 'Got him,' he said, and his voice was clearing. He pushed past the silent maids, down the stairs to the library. There he unlocked the safe and took a file out. He had one arm free to do it. Then, still carrying Gorjan, Lee went to the front door.

Margaret said feebly: 'Where are we going?'

'London—I told you. Walk.'

Somehow they made the garage and Lee opened the Bentley. Gasping, he got Gorjan in. He opened the other door.

'You sit with him in the back.'

'Mellion——'

'Get in. Don't talk.'

They had gone perhaps a mile when Margaret spoke again. 'Your nose,' she said.

'We'll fix it later.'

'I think it's been broken.'

'I know it.'

She was silent again as the miles slipped by. Gorjan, half lying, was breathing heavily. She felt his pulse again; she could feel it but only just. He was white as a detergent plug. Margaret asked unhappily: 'We're taking him back to the Hemmingway?'

Lee shook his head but he didn't turn it. 'We're going direct to London.'

'Where?'

'You'll soon find out.'

CHAPTER 12

Mellion Lee hadn't flattered himself that he had tied up Copeman well but he had hoped that it would hold him for an hour. That in fact was an underestimate. Lee mightn't lash like a seaman but he had struck hard and cleanly, and Copeman was still insensible when Robert Mortimer found him at ten o'clock. Major Mortimer cut him loose, and with patience and cold water brought him round. Copeman was shocked but he didn't seem fractured. He was also very angry; he'd walked blindly into a sucker-trap and his professional pride was hurt. No, he hadn't seen a thing.

Mortimer found milk and put it on the gas stove. Then he walked up to the house. Two frightened maids met him and he began to question them. But they hung their heads uncomfortably. They were evidently foreigners—Spanish or maybe wops. But which? Nothing was more fatal than to address a foreigner in a foreign language which didn't happen to be his own. You looked a fool and you put his back up. Robert Mortimer decided that he'd chance it. In his serviceable Italian he said gently: 'I'm not a policeman, you know.' It was true, he was thinking—strictly true.

The effect was immediate. The maids beamed happily and Mortimer was engulfed in a stream of the broadest Friuli. He let it flow over him, picking out the words he knew and piecing them together. There'd been a battlefield, a carnage, a scene of the utmost horror. Major Mortimer, making his discount, knew that somebody had been hurt. Had there, he asked, been weapons—pistols, for instance, or knives? The maids, with a faint impatience, shook their heads, and the younger recovered first. But the furniture had been smashed to bits, the *signore* must really visit it, the mirrors, the chairs, the wardrobe too, the room had been struck by the wrath of God, worse than anything in Naples (she crossed herself expertly) and the blood, *signore*, a river of blood, it had been horrible, a slaughterhouse, properly a slaughterhouse. . . .

She stopped to draw breath and the other took the running up. Mortimer had heard enough. 'Ladies,' he said. 'Esteemed and gentle ladies.'

There was a split second of silence and Mortimer seized it. . . . And who was fighting who?

The *padrone* and the other man.

What other man?

The guest—that Slav. (They used the word which in dialect meant siave too.)

Who won?

The *padrone* won. But he was covered of blood, he——

What happened then?

The *padrone* picked the slave up. The slave was dead.

Dead? Are you sure?

Well. . . .

Where did he carry him?

Down to the car. And the woman went with him. They all drove away.

Do you know where they went?

And how should we know that?

But Mortimer now had the story. He asked if he might use the telephone, receiving warm assurances that the house would be honoured if he would do so. He rang Colonel Russell and he gave him the essential: Gorjan, Mrs Palfrey and Mellion Lee had left. Together.

It was this call which had interrupted Russell as he was ending his interview with Nikola Mitrovic. His Excellency had risen but Russell waved him down again. With a scrupulous under-emphasis he said: 'Alex Gorjan has disappeared.'

The ambassador took it in total silence. Russell had always liked him but he'd never admired him more. He didn't protest and he didn't blame; he didn't waste time in questions. Instead he rose decidedly, holding his hand out. 'You'll be busy,' he said, 'so I'll leave you to work. If you'd give me a ring at tea-time——'

'I'll do that gladly.'

Nikola Mitrovic, Excellency and Plenipotentiary, ex-partisan and a very hard egg, went out. Russell watched his broad back, standing. When it had gone he sat down. This was a friend indeed.

Charles Russell began to telephone, and, twenty minutes later, he was taking the replies which his inquiries had set in train. The first was from James Scobell. . . . No, Lee hadn't been seen at his embassy and he hadn't gone back to his flat. . . . That was certain? Quite certain. But his Bentley was in its garage. He'd driven it there himself alone, giving his usual order that it be washed. He seemed to have caught a bloody nose but his manner had been normal. . . . There had been nothing inside the Bentley? No. Nor signs of a struggle.

Colonel Russell had thanked Mr James Scobell and two minutes later a different instrument rang. It was the area representative for South-West Ten and he'd had a piece of luck. His instructions had been to check on Mrs Palfrey's flat and dutifully he had done so. Number Forty-four Gilston Road was a Victorian house a little south of the fading splendours of the Boltons. It had been divided into flats and Margaret Palfrey had the top one. The owner of the middle was abroad, but on the ground floor there was an invalid ex-Indian Civilian. He went out very little so he liked to sit by the window. He saw a bit of life that way, he didn't feel so out of things. And at something around seven that morning he'd been drinking his morning tea. A car had drawn up, though he wouldn't be able to recognize it. But he'd recognized Mrs Palfrey and a man he'd noticed visiting her before. Yes, pretty regularly. This man had dragged another from the car, and together they had carried him inside. A drunk presumably. The first man had driven off again, returning in a taxi. The ex-Indian Civilian had been interested but he hadn't been astonished; he hadn't needed much pressing to advance his opinion that Mrs Palfrey was something below respectable. Now many years ago, in Poona it had been. . . .

Russell gave quick instructions. Get a man on the house and a tap on the telephone. . . . The man was on already? Good. Then work fast on the intercept.

He sat back awaiting a final call. It would be one from Gabriel Palliser, for he'd asked for an urgent interview. Soon it came through. The Minister would be free at noon. Charles Russell looked at the clock. He just had time for the single sheet of foolscap Palliser always asked for. And time for a second and vital call to the Milton Export and Import.

Mr Gabriel Palliser was less urbane than usual, but Russell, who respected him, could sympathize. This was something which no Minister could reasonably be expected to feel happy with. No, indeed. Palliser was saying curtly: 'It's a shambles.'

'I can see it's embarrassing politically.'

'That's the litotes of the century. Politically it's dynamite.' The Minister played with his gold cigarette case. 'Let's start at the beginning. Gorjan comes to England and somebody tries to kill him. We'll skip that for the moment and go on to phase two. Which began when our allies went after him. I told you about the start of that—I thought it was wise to do so—but I didn't then take it tragically. I thought they might make a mess of it, I feared they might even embarrass us. But I never dreamt of this. Gorjan goes down to Lee's country house, and it's clear Lee is ready to take dreadful risks. What do you think would have happened if your man hadn't found that file?'

'Presumably Lee would have used it. He'd have questioned Gorjan.'

'He might have got something out of him? The thing was on?'

'So Normer assures me. The brief had been done by a first-class scientist and Lee has the training to use it.'

The Minister considered it. 'But how? Why should Gorjan answer him?'

'I'd been asking myself just that.' Russell was feeling his way. 'Not torture,' he said, 'that's out. Lee's taking risks but I don't think he'd take that one.'

'I've heard stories about a truth drug.'

'Nonsense—or nonsense strictly. There's a whole group of drugs—pentothal is one of them—which depress the higher centres of the cortex. But they're tricky things to play with. If you don't give enough of them there's no effect at all, and if you administer a shade too much you send your man to sleep. You can sometimes make men babble but mostly it's rubbish. You can't guarantee the truth.'

'So you rule that right out?'

'Oh no—I wish I could. There's no truth drug in the sense that you can fill a hypodermic and a man will tell the truth on it, but there isn't any doubt that you can do things to the brain.' Russell's face was expressionless. Two men, he was thinking, in a cottage in Suffolk, two would-be murderers. Drugs hadn't been decisive but they'd been useful. He went on smoothly. 'But it's a delicate technique and very chancy. Nine times out of ten it doesn't work, but the tenth gives you something. Something. Not what a man must hide at all costs, not the straight confession which you might extract by torture, but if you're patient and have the time for it you can sometimes so condition him that he'll say what he otherwise wouldn't. People chatter after shock, you know. There's really nothing new in this—not in the principle. All that's new is the drugs which help you. And they aren't all depressants.'

'You think Lee could have them?'

'They weren't in his safe but you can carry a case of drugs. Mrs Palfrey was a doctor, too. Yes, I'd wondered and I was trying to check. But events went too fast for me.'

'And much too fast for *me*.' Mr Palliser thought again. 'Was Gorjan drugged when Lee took him off to London?'

'Not on the tale the maids told. Lee somehow discovered that my man had borrowed his briefing-file. He lay for him and slugged him, then he acted very quickly. He decided to run for London. It was anything but a cast-iron plan, but it was the only one available. He was bound to be discovered but it gave him a little time, and it got him away from the immediate attentions of a man he now knew was an agent. Maybe an English agent, maybe not. Whether he guessed that we knew he lived with Palfrey I can't say. I don't think that's important since in any case we'd have checked on her flat when she vanished from Nags Cottage. But she offered him a bolt-hole—very temporary but a bolt-hole.' For Colonel Russell it had been quite a speech; he drew a leisurely breath. 'So Lee tackles Gorjan and Gorjan doesn't like it. I wouldn't have liked it either. There was some sort of violence, and improbably Lee won it. There weren't any weapons and Gorjan's the more powerful man. But Lee leaves the house with Gorjan across his shoulders.' Russell allowed himself a well-timed pause. 'And what do you make of that?'

'Lee could have knocked him out.'

'Not according to the girls. Gorjan had Lee down and damned near out. Then suddenly Lee was up again. Gorjan was out.'

'Gorjan has been very ill.'

'I know.'

The Minister frowned and an ancient clock ticked heavily. Finally Palliser said: 'So it boils down to this. An American has used violence against an eminent foreign scientist. He has carried him off to his mistress's flat where they're all holed up together. There's very good evidence that the American means to ask the scientist questions which he shouldn't. That puts it, and deliberately, at the very lowest possible. He has rather less time than he may think he has, but any time's too much. And Gorjan's pretty sick again, that's certain. Suppose he dies?'

'I'd really rather not.'

'Hell, it could happen. Frankly, I'm frightened. Any scandal over Alex Gorjan and no one could see the end of it. I gather you're friendly with Mitrovic, which is very much just as well. You can hold him for a bit perhaps, but you can't keep him quiet for ever.'

'I promised to ring at tea-time.'

'Tea-time—four hours at most. And Gorjan apart, Lee's an official too. And nominally friendly. But there's been violence and there are witnesses.' Gabriel Palliser looked away; he asked doubtfully, clearly hating it: 'I suppose we could get a warrant?'

'Is that how you wish it handled?'

'No.' The Minister had exploded it. 'Any sort of publicity. . . . Quite fatal.' He recovered himself, a politician's disciplines propping an anxious man. 'I was hoping you'd have some suggestion.'

Charles Russell said cautiously: 'An idea had crossed my mind.'

'Any idea's a good one. Tell.'

'I've a very good friend called James Scobell. Scobell is an American, and that's essential. You won't know him, but he's the London representative of something you'll certainly have heard of. We always play ball when we're not competing, and we're not competing here. Rather to the contrary. Scobell, to put it bluntly, has been snubbed. Any move to exploit Gorjan should rightly have been handled by the people Scobell works for. And a very tough problem they'd have set us. Instead there's this Lee, a diplomat. Hell has no fury like a competent Intelligence agency obliged to watch a balls-up.' For the first time Russell smiled. 'Oh yes,' he said, 'Scobell would help us. I've just been telephoning.'

'How could he help us?'

'It's surprisingly simple—in my trade a good plan is.' Russell had begun to enjoy himself but the Minister hadn't.

'Please go on.'

'Scobell will take a taxi to Mrs Margaret Palfrey's flat. He'll ring the bell and perhaps they'll answer. If they don't he has certain skills. In either case he'll enter. Remember he's an American, so he'll conduct Mr Lee to his embassy. I doubt if there'll be violence again, but if there is Scobell hasn't just left the hospital. At the embassy Scobell has contacts; he knows he isn't loved there but he's unquestionably respected, and he'll be offering them the chance to scotch a scandal. He'll tell enough of the truth to remove Mellion Lee. Scobell doesn't dislike him personally but he loathes what he stands for—when it blunders and treads his toes down. There's an aircraft for America almost every hour round the clock. There's one at seven.' Russell was bland as a family priest. 'I happen to know that Scobell has booked a seat on it. Not in the Scobell name.'

'That would take care of part of it.' Palliser was impressed but not quite satisfied. 'And Gorjan?' he asked.

'I don't think Gorjan's a problem. Remove Mellion Lee, the possibility of a diplomatic rumpus, and Doctor Gorjan, besides being safe again, will be physically at our disposal. Two men of my own will be outside the Palfrey flat, and as soon as Scobell leaves with Lee they'll slip in quietly. What's against it? I'm tempted to go myself but I might be recognized. So my two men slip in and they collect Gorjan. I don't think the woman matters much. They take him—if you approve, that is—they take him to the Hemmingway.'

The Minister said promptly: 'I approve.'

'Then may I use your telephone?'

'Of course.'

Russell rang James Scobell but very briefly. As he put back the receiver Palliser said quietly: 'I'm really extremely grateful.'

'Thank James Scobell.'

'I'll be glad if you would. From me.'

Charles Russell walked back to the Security Executive. He was pleased that he seemed to have won a round but he was far from relaxing. Alex Gorjan was in England still and with luck he would remain so. Russell hadn't yet told his Minister of Mitrovic's proposal: there wasn't any point in it till Gorjan had been recovered. But if he stayed the Executive would inescapably be involved again. Alexander Gorjan would be Russell's sole responsibility, in a real sense his man. Within hours of his first arrival an attempt had been made to kill him. The same could be made again. Charles Russell shrugged. That had been normal, routine—almost, in its grim orthodoxy, decent. You killed a body to destroy a mind. But when you went for an invalid's brain itself, putting on the pressures, even using drugs on him though perhaps that hadn't happened yet, but risking a sick man's health and life, hounding him. . . .

Russell walked to his room and sat down. He had nothing to do till a call came through from James Scobell, then he'd telephone to Mitrovic in turn. He was grateful for the interval, for he was fighting an emotion which he did not wish to allow himself. He was angry—blind battle furious. He could have strangled Mellion Lee and he would cheerfully have framed him. Who, he remembered, would be flying away at seven. And that was a pity; that, though convenient, was something less than just. Russell had had a plan for Mellion Lee.

CHAPTER 13

Stevan Starc had slipped back to his West Indian railwayman knowing that he was in double trouble and that soon it might be triple. Back in his little room he checked his position grimly. First his masters intended to eliminate him. They had always known his hideout, indeed it was inconceivable that he would have been allowed to own such a thing without their knowledge, and now he was certain that of the various methods of dealing with a blown agent open to their pleasure it had pleased them to decide to kill him. The decision had taken four days but Starc hadn't been surprised at that. His masters were bureaucrats and he himself not wholly unimportant. His case would have gone to the capital, and in the capital four days was quick. He hadn't been unimportant and he'd failed; worse, he might talk. So they'd decided to erase him. In a sense he was almost relieved, for his masters must have considered an alternative to the simple choice of pulling him out or killing him. For instance they might have ordered him to confess. He must write to the police, make an affidavit perhaps (that sort of detail wouldn't have been forgotten) then walk into his embassy, demanding protection from his own ambassador. Stevan Starc almost smiled. That would fix Mitrovic, dirty the diplomatic waters finally. An admission of planning murder, the first Secretary of the Confederate Republic, the ridiculous British Foreign Office. . . . Christ, what a mess to gloat over: what a mess to exploit. It sounded a bit Byzantine but why not? His masters were Byzantium's heirs.

But that hadn't happened though it must have been weighed. Instead they were trying to get him. In the list of his difficulties that was easily first, but the second, if less dangerous, was ultimately as threatening. The English police were after him, and seriously too. That man from the café had said he was a policeman. Starc hadn't expected that so soon. He had noticed that his shirt was torn, but he couldn't be quite certain that he'd been recognized. He decided that wasn't important. The essential was that there had been police in the café at all, a policeman who, from his speech and manner, was certainly not a constable off duty. So senior plain-clothes police were active in North Four. That might be coincidence, but it was very unwise to play coincidences. And if it wasn't a coincidence it meant that the police were uncomfortably close to him. If the Poles didn't get him the policemen would.

Or, he remembered, the Security Executive. That was third on his list of dangers but by no means the least. He had been taught to despise the English police—poor oafs, they were shamefully fettered—but his instructors had had much respect for a certain Colonel Russell. Who held the two men he had sent to the Hemmingway, who in time was bound to break them. Not at once, for the English didn't torture much. But if their techniques of interrogation weren't slavishly old-fashioned nor were they ineffective. Once his two men talked, once they positively connected him with the attempt on Gorjan, he'd be known as a dangerous agent of an unfriendly foreign Power. The Executive might leave it to the police at first, but if the police failed to find him they'd act themselves. And the Executive weren't policemen. That had been impressed on him.

Once those two men talked. . . . For all he knew they'd talked by now. Stevan Starc swung his legs from the narrow bed. He began to clean his gun.

Detective Inspector Mellor, fettered oaf, carried no gun; he carried authority and a lifetime's experience. His Superintendent had drawn a quarter-mile circle on a map, telling him to beat it house by house. Mellor hadn't laughed at him but afterwards he had. That was the sort of thing a Super said, a Super who'd been sitting on his arse too long. It could no doubt be done but it would take a regiment and, more important, it would take at least a month. Detective Inspector Mellor didn't have a month but he still had his first idea. He'd decided to stick to it. Thieves—West Indian thieves especially. He was an experienced policeman and this wasn't his manor, but he had been shocked that in the quarter-mile circle there were a hundred and twenty-six known criminals and that ninety-three of these weren't in any sense natives of England. He had begun on the ninety-three. He could now call formally for the help of the Division in whose area he was operating and his own men had been reinforced. He had reduced his list to twenty and today was his birthday. It was a fine clear morning and he was allowing himself an unusual optimism. He was lucky on his birthdays.

But not in his problem, which geographically was difficult. In most of the area you could call at a house, and provided you watched the back of it there wasn't much chance that your man could get away. But this house was different. It was one in a row of what had once been artisans' cottages, now verging on slumdom though not yet officially. The row formed the west side of a quadrilateral of jumbled buildings, the south facing Fonthill Road. There wouldn't have been a problem if the houses had been back-to-backs, but in the centre of the untidy mass was a complex of little workshops. They were gear-cutting shops and chainmakers, the type of light industry attracting small notice but cosy profits, and they were tangled together in a lush promiscuity. Mellor had made his recce., deciding at once that it would be impossible to picket them individually. Nor did he wish to. He saw his quarry as a rabbit in a cornfield. You reaped the field inwards till only a small patch stood. Then you put in a couple of reliable old dogs, and it was astonishing what they flushed for you.

So he wouldn't be over-subtle; he'd walk up to the house and ring the bell. This particular West Indian was virtuously married—Mellor had checked that too—and his wife didn't work. Once in he'd look round and today was his birthday. If a policeman's gods remembered him he'd find a hastily vacated room. He wouldn't find Starc but that was all right; he'd find papers perhaps, or a bottle of stain, enough to reassure him. Starc would have slipped away, down one wall, over another, somewhere into the busy jungle which lay behind him. And that was all right too. The quadrilateral was framed by four cleared streets, and at each corner Mellor had posted a police car. There were men in plain clothes patrolling between the cars. He'd beat out the workshops at leisure, for now he'd have plenty of time.

Mellor was sufficiently confident to have permitted himself the luxury of speculation. . . . Which side would Starc break? Not to the south, he thought. Starc would want to hide not race for it, and Fonthill Road offered nothing to hide in; it just went on and on, an interminable squalor. And not to the west. The cottage itself faced west. Starc's hunters would have entered by the soiled front door, and a man, unlike an animal, would seldom double back against the beat.

Which left north and east and the north side was out. There was cover there, true, for across the street the ground rose steeply in the embankment of a railway. It was a siding for coal and for the lorries of a fish business. A bridge connected it, across the road, with the main line railway station, and the embankment was overgrown with sooty alder. It would be tempting but it wasn't on. For at the bottom of the embankment was a stout wooden fence. It wasn't more than a shoulder high, an active man could scramble it, but at the top was barbed wire, four strands on wooden posts. That too might be negotiated by a man with time and wire-cutters. Starc might have the second but he wouldn't have the first.

So he'd break to the east and he'd sprint for the Underground. It was a warren of stairs and passages, one of the most complicated Undergrounds in London. Once safely inside it a man would have a very fair chance of losing his pursuers. A long subway led to it but Mellor had three good men there. He walked round the quadrilateral once again, checking his dispositions. Then he went to the cottage and rang the bell.

Stevan Starc had been expecting him. One of the advantages of his carefully chosen hideout was a skylight on to the long flat roof which joined the terraced cottages, and Starc had been keeping watch behind the surprisingly elegant parapet. He had worked out a brick and could watch without exposing himself. He had noticed that the street was unusually empty, then the police cars at its corners, finally the plain-clothes dicks, absurdly self-consciously strolling. You could never mistake a plain-clothes copper. Stevan Starc snarled and waited. He too thought he'd plenty of time.

For his assessment hadn't been so different from Mellor's. Caught in this quadrilateral no man would break south, nor west against the men who hunted him. He'd go for the east since the north was impossible.

Except that it wasn't—Stevan Starc had seen to that. If he could get up that embankment he could lose a hundred policemen. For one thing they wouldn't be expecting it, and even if by some ill chance they had posted a man at the top Starc, if he had to, would shoot. Then over the bridge, across the tracks, and on to the first of a file of platforms. Down the steps to a tunnel and at once you were in a maze. There were a ticket-collector and a barrier, but the barrier was vaultable, then a circular stair to the Northern. It was the terminus here, the blind line down to Moorgate. Two platforms and in the rush-hour trains from both. Or if you were unlucky here you weren't by a long chalk finished. Up another flight of stairs and to the subway. They'd have men at its mouth but you'd be fifty yards behind them. Turn right, twenty yards, then to the right again. More stairs and the main Northern now. Two tracks again and trains going both ways.

Stevan Starc knew for he had reconnoitred carefully. If he could reach the embankment. . . . They wouldn't be expecting that, conceding him the initiative. They wouldn't be expecting it—the wire was impassable. Or had been until he'd fixed it. He had slipped out in the small hours, severing it near the uprights, joining it loosely with ordinary wire. There hadn't been much tension and the job had been quite straightforward. It would have been difficult to spot the join even if it were known. So you took with you a good strong stick. You put the stick firmly against the strands; you pushed and you jumped. The paling alone was nothing.

Stevan Starc heard the bell ring and went down to his room. He had plenty of time, but it was a mistake to despise your enemies, or at least to despise excessively. He took his gun and he took his stick; he took gloves too, since there was no point in risking injury. Then he opened the window and dropped quietly to the ground. . . . Between two crumbling outhouses and over a little wall. It was the passage behind the chainmaker's but the windows looked away from it. He found a back door and tried it. Open. He stepped into a sudden noise and through it. One or two men looked up but didn't challenge him. They weren't being paid to challenge strangers. Across the yard and into the office. A girl was sitting typing and he waved at her. 'I'm a new boy,' he said. 'We'll meet.' His voice was steady but not his heart. Through the last of the doors, then the gate to the road. . . . Up the embankment. Out.

Stevan Starc stopped. There were police cars at every corner and in any other country they'd be armed. Machine pistols probably, for this was clearly a considerable operation. They'd have him in cross-fire, a murderous enfilade. Here all he had to watch for was an unarmed plain-clothes dick. It had all been explained to him a dozen times. Nevertheless. . . .

He made himself open the gate.

At once a man jumped him, trying for the policeman's antiquated arm lock. Starc countered smoothly, catching the man's right hand and bending it. He held the wrist in both his hands, then swung the whole arm in the wrestler's Irish whip. The man didn't go with it and Starc heard the arm crack. The policeman didn't utter; he stood dumbly, incredulous, his right arm hanging uselessly. They'd never taught him that one and he was thinking it was unfair.

Starc was across the road, instinctively bending double. From the police cars men were running but he had sixty yards on both of them. That was sixty yards in police boots—call it ten seconds. He was up on the paling, holding his stick in front of him. He threw himself forward and for an instant nothing happened. He'd rewired it too tight, he'd bungled. . . .

Suddenly the four strands went. Starc jerked himself sideways away from them, falling in a clumsy heap. The pause had unbalanced him and he'd cut himself badly. But at once he was up again. He thrust through the alder, stumbling on a decade's débris. Behind him were futile police whistles but above was the siding. He reached it on all fours, straightening, tripping again on a hidden root, cracking his head cruelly on an untidy pile of coal. A railwayman stared and a man on a fish truck shouted. Starc ran across the bridge, ducking below the cast-iron sides. Even the English must shoot by now. But no shot came. He reached the first platform, diving down the stairway. The tunnel now and almost home. On his left was the barrier. He jumped but he missed his vault. He fell again shatteringly but somehow got up. The elderly ticket inspector was trying to speak and failing. In forty years' service he'd never seen the like of it. Starc stumbled down the spiral stair. He was dizzy with punishment and forced himself to slow. He couldn't afford another fall. If there wasn't a train he'd just about had it. Hell, he was going to faint. If there wasn't a train he'd never get farther. Not to the other line. There were two sets of stairs again, one up, one down. . . .

The train was just leaving. The doors were shutting but with the last of his strength Starc reached them. He put out his foot and a porter swore. For a moment there was nothing, then a reluctant hiss of air. The doors opened slowly and Starc slipped inside.

For two stations he sat motionless, eyes shut. Then he lit a cigarette, inhaling hungrily. He got out at Old Street and volunteered his fare. A taxi was cruising. Stevan Starc gave the driver an address in Gilston Road.

There was one place he could go still and he'd kept the lady's key.

CHAPTER 14

At Forty-four Gilston Road they had carried Gorjan to the bedroom. Margaret was moving in what she would have liked to think a dream. She knew that it was not. Lee had overwhelmed her, sweeping protest aside imperiously. She hadn't in fact tried much of it. This was quite outside experience and she was frightened. She was frightened of a dozen things but Lee she feared most.

She had felt Gorjan's pulse and now she was straightening. Gorjan was breathing heavily but presently he stirred. Margaret said uneasily: 'I think he's coming round.'

'That's good.'

'A doctor,' she said, not hopefully. 'I'll telephone a doctor.'

'You're the doctor.' Lee felt in his pocket, handing her a leather case.

'What's this?'

'Why don't you look and see?'

She opened the little box. Inside was a hypodermic and, packed carefully in recesses, three rows of drug capsules. She picked one out at random, reading the label.

'Pentothal!'

'You've heard of it?'

'It does things to the brain. Psychiatrists sometimes use it when they happen to be doctors too. It makes patients talk, or so they say. But it's terribly tricky stuff. I wouldn't dare use it.'

'You're lucky,' he said. 'You're not going to have to.'

Gorjan had opened his eyes.

'I don't understand.'

Lee said indifferently: 'I was going to make Gorjan talk, or rather I meant to try. I was going to ask him questions—you were going to give the pentothal. Now you won't have to. But there's an ordinary barbiturate in that case you've got and I think we're going to need it.'

'Mellion——'

'Be quiet.'

Lee was watching Gorjan. Gorjan had rolled his head away. He was sweating and grey, evidently in dreadful pain. He said thickly, his eyes shut again: 'Where am I?'

'In London. In Mrs Palfrey's flat.'

'But why?'

'You've had another breakdown. Mrs Palfrey is a doctor.'

Alexander Gorjan groaned.

'I'd like to ask you some questions. Just a few questions.'

Gorjan said faintly: 'Hospital. . . .'

'Not yet. Just a few questions first.'

With an appalling effort Gorjan asked: 'What about?'

'Your work.'

'My work! Go to hell.'

'I think you're a very foolish man. I can see you're in agony and I told you Mrs Palfrey was a doctor. She has drugs in that case—release.' Lee's voice was quiet and soothing. 'Release. Just a question or two and an end of pain.'

Gorjan didn't answer. He was greyer than ever, breathing in gasps which shook him.

Margaret Palfrey had begun to cry.

'And afterwards hospital. You may die if we don't take you there.'

Alex Gorjan was somehow sitting up. His lower lip was bleeding where he had bitten almost through it. But he hadn't been defeated. 'We'll get you,' he said savagely. He fell back in a final collapse. Mellion Lee shook his shoulder, gently at first, then brutally. Margaret through her tears said weakly: 'Mellion, he may die.'

'Shut up.'

'Mell——'

Mellion Lee raised his hand but dropped it. He'd lost and he wasn't used to it. He began to laugh but the sound was hollow.

The Security Executive prided itself that it never gave orders which the recipient couldn't obey, and the man who was watching Margaret Palfrey's flat had had instructions which were well within the practical. Anybody who looked normal, a milkman, for instance, or the man to read the meters, was to be allowed to make his call, but someone who looked suspicious was to be stopped if it were possible. Not stopped at all costs—that wasn't an order which Russell often gave—but stopped if he could be. There were police within call and the watcher was to use his own discretion.

He hadn't had a second's doubt about the man who was now approaching. He looked utterly disreputable. Stevan Starc had left his taxi in the Fulham Road and was walking up to Margaret Palfrey's flat. He hadn't renewed his face stain since it hadn't been worth the trouble, but his clothes were in tatters where the wire had ripped them, he was black with the alders' ancient soot, and at every tenth pace he staggered on an ankle he now realized he had sprained. When he came to the steps of Margaret's house a man appeared from nowhere. Starc hadn't noticed him. The man said politely: 'Were you calling at Flat Three?'

Stevan Starc nodded.

'Would you mind if I asked what for?'

'Why should you?'

'I've had certain instructions.'

They were standing where the steps began, Starc on the first of them. He had turned when accosted, his back to the front door. The other was facing it, one step below. Starc said to him pleasantly: 'Instructions, eh? So you must be a policeman.' He pulled out a pocket handkerchief, mopping his face, returning it to his pocket casually. His hand came out again in a lightning and practised draw. The watcher was looking at a gun he didn't recognize. Stevan Starc spoke again: 'I'm going backwards up those steps. The front door may be locked but I've the key to that too. I must show you my back as I use it, but I can turn before you can make six steps and reach me. Or is it seven? And I've very good hearing. Right?'

The other didn't answer.

Starc began to walk backwards, his gun hand moving smoothly as his body rose, five degrees depression for each step. He was thinking again that this was England. Anywhere else the man would be armed; he'd put a bullet through his vertebrae the second he turned his back. But here. . . .

He swung quickly but unafraid. No unarmed man would rush him up seven steps. He had the keys out already, both of them on a ring, and he unlocked the door left-handed. He slipped inside and shut and locked it, limping up the stairs to Margaret's flat, opening it with the other key. The fussy living-room was empty and he walked into the bedroom.

Starc stopped in his tracks. There was a man on the bed and he saw it was Alex Gorjan. He was unconscious or maybe dead. Beyond the bed was another man he recognized. They had sometimes met at parties in the days when it hadn't been distasteful to be cuckolding an American dear colleague. They seemed a very long time ago. On the nearside of the bed stood Margaret Palfrey. She had been facing away but she turned as she heard him. Her mouth dropped open in the unconscious gape he hated.

'Stevan. . . .'

Stevan Starc ignored her, speaking to Mellion Lee. 'Mr Mellion Lee?' He still held the gun.

'How do you know my name?'

'We've met before. I'm Stevan Starc, in the Confederate Embassy.'

Incredulity chased astonishment across Lee's face. He hadn't recognized Starc and he flatly disbelieved him. This tattered and filthy gunman. . . .

'I don't believe a word of it.'

'Ask Mrs Palfrey.'

'Well?'

Margaret said unhappily: 'He is.'

'Very well, so she knows you. But how did you get in here?'

'I still have a key.'

For a moment it didn't register, then Mellion Lee flushed deeply. He stared at Margaret Palfrey and he began to move round the bed. Starc flicked the gun at him.

'Not yet—you can beat her later. That is, if I don't.' With his free hand he pointed at Gorjan. 'That's Alex Gorjan. Is he dead?'

Lee shook his head.

'Then why is he here? What are you doing with him?'

Lee didn't answer.

Starc turned on Margaret Palfrey. 'Talk,' he said. 'Fast.'

There was a second's hesitation and an uncertain glance at Mellion Lee. Then it all came out in a craven fright. Gorjan had been asked to the cottage in the country. Nothing had happened till this morning, then Lee had carried him off to London. Yes, by force. There'd been a fight and Gorjan had collapsed. . . . Why had he been brought to London? She didn't know, she wasn't in this, she really wasn't, but there'd been some stupid idea of questioning him. . . . What sort of questions? She didn't know, Gorjan had come round but hadn't lasted.

Margaret, if she had known it, was doing the worst thing possible. Starc was looking at her with an expression she'd never seen. A decent reticence he would have respected and courage he admired. If he'd had to beat it out of her. . . . But no, she was spilling shamelessly. This babbling broken woman made him sick. He asked coldly: 'Then you had nothing to do with this?'

'Nothing, I swear it. Stevan——'

'What's that in your hand?'

She looked down uncertainly. She was holding the leather case still but she'd quite forgotten it.

'What's that in your hand?'

'Stevan, I——'

'Drop it.'

The case fell to the ground and opened. Starc stared silently at the spilled contents. He bent and picked a capsule up. Pentothal. He'd heard of it.

. . . She was a duty he'd been assigned to. He had the contempt of his faith for the irritating word progressive, but it was a political fact that those who blared progress loudest were also the most naïve. It was easy to subvert them to a system which would have sickened their pale muddled minds if they had troubled to understand it. Sometimes they worked knowingly and sometimes one simply deceived them. But their potential for minor treason was unlimited—no communist dared neglect it. So he'd been assigned to Margaret Palfrey and she'd been fooling him all the time. She'd been working for his enemies, for Mellion Lee, American. Pentothal and questioning. Margaret had been a doctor once—all that fellow-travelling nonsense had been a sham. She'd utterly deceived him, humiliating him intolerably. Moreover it shouldn't have happened. An axiom should have saved him and it could hardly be a simpler one. Lee was very wealthy and an intellectual Leftie would do anything for cash.

Stevan Starc shuddered. He was filthy and knew it, a scarecrow. But a bath and fresh clothes would take care of mere dirt. Now he felt unclean, unclean. He wanted to vomit. Having to go to bed with her, the avid shameless thing, the far Left conversation first, the baby talk after.

He raised the gun deliberately and Margaret was at the end of it. From behind the bed Lee rushed him. Starc fired and Lee fell.

Starc had sat down to think. Margaret was fussing with bandages and a bowl, dropping the first and slopping the second. She was astonishingly maladroit. Starc was thinking that he'd seen all this before. The irony amused him but he hadn't time to savour it. He said to her shortly: 'Relax. He isn't badly hurt. I only shot to stop him. You'll find a wound in the shoulder.'

Margaret had worked Lee's coat off. He had opened his eyes but he wasn't moving. Starc was maddened by her fumbling but his private rage was spent. He must take a great decision and the risk of it appalled him. He sat for a little longer, silent, weighing what he knew was now inevitable. It was in fact his only chance—chance for his life and perhaps for his future.

If he delivered up Gorjan alive it would be triumph snatched from entire disaster.

He walked into the living-room, ringing a house in Highgate Village. When a recognized voice replied he said: 'Rickoff? Starc here.'

There was a second of shocked silence, then instant protest. 'You must be insane. This is an open line. You were told never, in any circumstances——'

'It's desperately important.'

'Why?'

Starc said: 'Gorjan——' and the line began to rasp at him. There was a faulty connection or possibly they were tapping it. He shook the receiver angrily and it repaid him with a continuous howl. This time he shouted.

'Gorjan——'

'I can't hear a thing.'

'Gorjan——'

There was sudden silence again as inexplicably the line cleared. The voice at the other end said quickly:

'I heard just one word. A name. *You're not to repeat it.'*

There was another long pause and Starc had to ask:

'Are you still there?'

'I am. Where are you?'

'I'm at Forty-four Gilston Road.'

'Whose house is that?'

'It's Mrs Margaret Palfrey's flat. The top one.'

'Yes, I've heard of Mrs Palfrey.'

There was a final silence as Rickoff thought. At last he said: 'At midnight tonight. The car will be a grey one.'

He was gone.

The man who was watching in Gilston Road been undecided. He had been held up at pistol-point, and in his long but not particularly distinguished service with the Security Executive that had happened to him twice before. He hadn't been blamed in either case, for his superiors were fair-minded men and he hadn't himself been armed. But there had been something about his colleagues' manner. They hadn't raised eyebrows and far less laughed, indeed they had shown their sympathy. But it had been a special sort of sympathy and it hadn't been easy to take. A third dose would be poison.

So he had been hesitating when he heard the shot. The noise had been muffled but he had been half expecting it. That made up his mind for him. He ran for the police car, discreetly parked, and at once was on the radio. It had been netted to the Executive and Russell himself answered. When the outside man had finished Russell asked: 'You're certain you heard a shot?'

'Quite certain. It wasn't loud enough to attract attention, but the man who broke in was armed and I was listening.'

'Did you recognize this man?'

'I can't be sure, sir. I've an impression I've seen a photograph but the background was quite different. It was a well-dressed respectable man, not a thug with a gun.'

'Do you remember the name on the photograph?'

'No, sir.'

'Where did you see it?'

'In one of our files, but I can't be sure which.'

'Make a guess. I won't hold it against you.'

'I've an idea. . . . The file for the diplomats.'

'Wait.' There was a teletype police report on Russell's desk and he had been reading it with interest. It seemed to have been quite a morning in North Four. Stevan Starc was at large again. Russell re-read two paragraphs of the report. 'Were this man's clothes torn?'

'Yes.'

'Did he seem to have been in trouble?'

'He was lame and very dirty.'

'I think that will do—I'm *afraid* that will do.' Charles Russell thought briefly. 'Stay on the job and I'll send you a reinforcement. If this man leaves the house you're to follow him. Otherwise stay clear of it. Don't risk another shooting. Understood?'

'Understood, sir.'

Russell looked at his watch and frowned. At any minute Scobell would be leaving for Gilston Road. And now he mustn't —he mustn't indeed. That plan was dead.

Russell rang the Milton Export and Import Company. He caught James Scobell but only just. Scobell listened silently, then said: 'But this has rather changed things.'

'You're very English this morning.'

'But seriously. You say this Starc was armed?'

'He was. It could have been Lee shooting but I doubt it.'

'So do I. So who did Starc shoot?'

'Gorjan, I'm afraid. Who else? He's tried for him once already and this must have looked a pushover.'

Scobell thought it over. 'And how did Starc get to Gilston Road?'

'I don't know that yet.'

'And perhaps it's a side issue.' There was a pause, then reluctant judgement. 'My friend, we're in trouble. All of us. Mellion Lee is there too. So it's murder of eminent scientist in American diplomat's love-nest. The diplomat was a witness. Why? In the morning at that.' Scobell reflected again; he said at last: 'I could still go to Gilston Road.'

'Risking shooting it out?'

'Maybe.'

'Suppose Starc gets *you*.'

'Suppose.'

'No.' Russell was final. 'That simply risks two stiffs for one.' He contrived a laugh but it wasn't merry. 'We've got to think this out again. Can you get down here quickly? I'll ask Mitrovic too.'

Scobell said: 'I've started.'

CHAPTER 15

The Minister's private secretary looked at what the typist had just finished. He had ordered it as a matter of urgency. He could perfectly well have done it himself since he wasn't a bad typist, but it was inconceivable that a member of the administrative grade should do his own typing. So he had sent for a stenographer. Ten precious minutes had been irrevocably lost but the traditions remained inviolate. He looked carefully at the typing. The meeting had been arranged with what the private secretary considered entirely indecent haste, but that wasn't a reason to do things less than properly. There wouldn't be an agenda—Gabriel Palliser had declined the suggestion brusquely—but it sounded a very odd gathering and not everybody present might know everybody else. So the private secretary had made a little list of those whom his Minister had inexplicably invited. There were five copies: one for the Minister, one for each visitor, and one for himself. He had been told that a note of the meeting wouldn't be required but he was determined to attend it just the same. One couldn't have one's Minister indulging in secret meetings. Now he read through the list:

The Minister

Yes, that was correct. In his own splendid room Mr Palliser was The Minister. It sounded more impressive too:

His Excellency M. Nikola Mitrovic
Ambassador Extraordinary and Plenipotentiary to the Confederate Republic

The private secretary looked at this with a certain doubt. It was 'to' which was worrying his finicky Wykehamist intelligence. Was it 'to' or 'for' or even plain 'of'? It was possible that complete correctitude demanded 'Ambassador to' but 'Plenipotentiary of'. In normal circumstances he would have telephoned to the Protocol Department of the Foreign Office, but this afternoon there wasn't time. He frowned in a kind of pain, for he had the compulsion of his calling to get it right at all costs. The details, of course: a couple of noughts misplaced was nothing. What was Exchequer and Audit for? And he bitterly resented that he hadn't had time to telephone. A Minister who behaved like this, slapping on meetings at no notice at all, was an impossible man to work for. And sharp—sometimes rude. Not a man one could think of as a colleague. The private secretary frowned again, deciding finally for 'to'. He wouldn't have cared to be pressed for reasons, but 'of' and 'for' seemed vaguely commonplace:

Colonel Charles Russell

That at least was easy. The private secretary knew what Charles Russell did, for the head of the Executive reported first to his own Minister. But his name appeared in no list of officials. It would have been wholly incorrect to add his job:

Mr James Scobell
Managing Director of the Milton Export & Import Agency, Ltd.

This time the frown was a scowl. Now what could a businessman be doing in a meeting of high officials? This was quite without precedent and therefore suspect. The private secretary's nose was long and thin and curious, and now it twitched involuntarily. All right, he'd soon find out.

He went through the connecting door and into his Minister's room. Palliser was sitting in a leather armchair. His eyes were shut but he wasn't asleep, and the private secretary sensed his tension. He went to the table and began to arrange five chairs, putting before each of them a copy of his paper. When he had finished he coughed discreetly.

'Five minutes to half-past two. Everything is ready.'

Palliser opened his eyes. 'Thank you,' he said pleasantly. He looked at the table and his expression changed. 'Five places?' he asked.

'Yourself, the ambassador, Colonel Russell——'

'I can count up to four.'

The private secretary went back to his office a very angry young prig indeed. That man a Minister! What was Whitehall coming to? No note of a meeting, not trusting your officials, *secrecy*. . . . The proceeding was dangerous—no, worse. The private secretary found the worst word he knew. The whole affair was irregular.

The meeting had been fixed at Russell's suggestion, and when the head of the Executive asked for an urgent meeting it was business. Palliser had agreed at once. Russell had told him that he would be consulting first with James Scobell and Mitrovic, and as the three men came in Russell introduced Scobell. He called him James Scobell, no more, but the Minister had a graceful word about the importance of imports and exports. They all sat round the table.

Forty minutes later it was satisfactorily decided. Russell had begun by putting a tape-recorder on the table, playing back to Gabriel Palliser the interrupted conversation between Starc and Rickoff. . . . The Minister would have heard of Rickoff? Yes, Russell had imagined it. And the other speaker was Stevan Starc, who'd been causing them all embarrassment. His own ambassador especially. Russell had run the tape twice for honest measure, then produced the single sheet of foolscap which was the passport to the Minister's good opinion of any official. He had written it hurriedly and he wasn't very proud of it. Given a little more time he could have polished it considerably, but he flattered himself that at least it was clear. Gabriel Palliser picked it up.

'May I take it this comes from all of you?'

'You may.'

The Minister began to read.

1. *We have started from two assumptions*:
A. *That Stevan Starc has shot Gorjan. Other explanations of the firing can be imagined, but since Starc was under*

103

orders to kill Gorjan and had already tried to do so they seem excessively optimistic.

B. That having succeeded in his mission Rickoff is now prepared to extricate Starc. That again is not explicit. The two of them were talking on an open line and were necessarily being cautious. But it is a fact that Rickoff is sending a car to Gilston Road at midnight.

2. We therefore start from the fact of murder and we cannot compound a felony. That is not because my organization has unexpectedly acquired an over-tender conscience for the law but because any attempt at concealment would be too dangerous. Lee was in the flat, as was Mrs Margaret Palfrey, and either could give the lie to any story which was not true. Therefore the basic limitation on any plan now possible is that Starc must be arrested first.

The Minister looked at Nikola Mitrovic. 'You've accepted that?' he asked.

'I'm reluctantly obliged to, but you can see where it's going to lead. The best scientist in my country has been murdered by my First Secretary. Once there's a trial in open court. . . .'

'Oh quite. But a politically slanted trial wouldn't suit our own book either, so I'll do what I can about the way they handle motive. It will be up to the Law Officers but Benson's a good friend of mine.'

'You're really extremely kind.'

'I can see you're in a horrid hole.'

His Excellency hid a smile behind his formidable moustache. He had a very good ear for the English tongue and he had recognized this as a Minister's way of talking, not an official's. Officials had a language of their own, and to succeed in Whitehall you must learn to use it properly. You must be clear but not too lucid: being too lucid was considered a sort of arrogance. And a word like horrid would decidedly have been suspect. Awkward yes, but hardly horrid. And the Minister never made little jokes, cosy little allusive jokes which dear colleagues would understand. He could be cynical, even witty, but he never played the meeting. He was a Minister of the Crown, one of the more powerful ones, but in the British civil service he would certainly have gone nowhere. So much the better since he was capable of decision still.

Palliser had gone back to Russell's paper.

3. Starting from the essential that Starc must be arrested we can see two courses open:

A. The orthodox course is to send police into the Palfrey flat. In the circumstances you may feel they should be armed. Since Starc is clearly desperate, that risks a gun fight in Gilston Road.

The Minister looked up again. 'Gilston Road,' he said reflectively. 'We can't chance another siege of Sidney Street.' He returned to the paper.

> *B. The second course is a variation of the original plan that Scobell should enter Mrs Palfrey's flat. He would have removed Mr Lee, whereafter we would have taken Gorjan to hospital. Gorjan is now dead, but the problem of Mr Lee remains. We have therefore considered the possibility of allowing Rickoff to remove Starc freely, at any rate from the area of Gilston Road.*

Advantages of this course

1. It obviates any shooting in the centre of London.
2. It will allow one of two scandals to be suppressed, since once Starc is out of the flat Scobell could still put the original plan into effect to the extent of removing Mellion Lee and conducting him to his embassy. Lee's own actions against Gorjan have made him political dynamite and we imagine you would prefer that he didn't explode in England.

Disadvantages of this course

But the Minister had put the paper down. 'The disadvantages speak for themselves.' He glanced again at the sheet of foolscap, ' "Allowing Rickoff to remove Starc freely, at any rate from the area of Gilston Road." But suppose he got much further?' Gabriel Palliser looked at Russell.

'It's a condition of the second course that they do get *some* way further. You can take it we shouldn't aim to stop them in a crowded London street—that would immediately defeat one of Course B's advantages. We'll have to let them get clear of London. Whereafter Starc will be arrested by perfectly ordinary policemen. Perfectly ordinary but especially discreet. Any other persons with him, any foolishness with firearms, will be a matter for myself. That's why the policemen will be especially reliable.'

'Suppose they take him to their embassy?'

'It's conceivable but I doubt it. Embassies are technically foreign territory—inside their walls a man is safe—but you still have to get him out again.' Russell turned to James Scobell. 'You've had experience yourselves, I think.'

'We have indeed.' Scobell spoke sourly. It had been a politically minded cleric and they'd been stuck with him properly. They couldn't even trade him since he wasn't their own citizen.

'Then where do you think they'll head for?' It was Palliser again. 'A dash for a ship or aircraft?'

'Or a launch on a lonely beach. The ship would be standing off.'

'You feel confident of stopping them?'

'We'll be following on a level start.'

'There's a risk, though?'

'There always is.'

The Minister considered through most of a cigarette. James Scobell was thinking too. Go to a meeting, lawyers or civil servants, and they nattered interminably, tentative and ambiguous. But go to the top and, if you could get there, men talked your own language. And often rather better. James Scobell thought of Washington. There were men there who could have panicked and they couldn't be justly blamed. Two foreign diplomats in different but equally destructive scandals, the traditional enemy apparently operating as freely in your capital as he did in some satellite. Very strong nerves could stretch forgivably. But Palliser. . . .

Gabriel Palliser had risen. 'Course B,' he said. 'Good luck.' He shook hands with all of them.

. . . An extraordinary people and dangerously deceptive. It had been a mistake to destroy their empire quite so ruthlessly.

Russell, Mitrovic and James Scobell walked back to the Security Executive. Mitrovic drank some slivovich, then slipped away quietly. He wasn't insensitive and he knew that the other two would wish to talk alone. There was nothing more he could do himself. When he had gone Russell looked at his watch.

'I've had much less time to plan in.'

'So have I.'

They smiled comfortable smiles, rivals in a necessary alliance. It was the happiest of relationships and perhaps the most fruitful. Russell began to talk and Scobell listened. From time to time he made a suggestion. Russell listened in turn, nodding agreement or quietly rejecting. When he rejected he gave a good reason. They were equals and quite at ease, and when they had finished both knew it without saying so. Russell picked up a telephone, telling his secretary that he wanted six men together. As soon as they were ready they were to be netted into the intercom.

She said it would take ten minutes.

Right.

He used the interval briefly to write. He wrote in short paragraphs and Scobell saw there were six of them. Presently the intercom buzzed.

'All on the net, sir.'

Russell picked up his notes, beginning to read. He read slowly, his quiet voice level. At the end he asked simply: 'Are there any questions?'

There were two and he answered both. Then he switched off. James Scobell said without pomposity: 'We've done everything humanly possible.'

'That still leaves us human.'

Rickoff had been sending some very urgent signals to his capital. It would have been possible to use the radio-telephone, but to do so would have exposed him to precisely the same rebuke he had administered to Starc, even though voice radio was heavily scrambled and supposedly secure. But one could never be quite certain, and the capital had an almost mystical mistrust of telephones of all kinds. So he had used the high-speed radio and he had sent in code. He was confident of its security. Even the superbly sophisticated computers of the National Security Agency wouldn't have broken this code, and that for a very good reason. It had only been used once before. He could use it a third time and then they would withdraw it. That wasn't enough for a feed.

His first message had been simple: Alexander Gorjan was now in a place from which it might be possible to remove him alive. Rickoff had asked for orders. That was all.

He did not receive them. Instead, an hour later, he was looking at twenty questions. He was neither irritated nor surprised, for he was an official himself and he had worked in headquarters. Put up a solid plan to them, complete, and the odds were they'd turn it down. But whet their curiosity, let them make the running, and at least you stood a chance on it. Officials didn't differ much whatever their nationality.

He answered the questions meticulously and, an hour later again, received his answer. There were things which could be done in London and things which could not. The risk was unacceptable. *Niet*.

It was the answer he had expected and he had already prepared his own. It had needed careful drafting but he had done the same thing before. In effect he said, though not in words, that though he mightn't be quite at the top of the Bureau he had very good friends from other days in positions which gave it orders. Gorjan alive would be a prize without price, far beyond the original modest target that he be killed. To turn down even the chance of it was a great responsibility. If later the decision was queried. . . .

It was delicately done, innuendo and allusion, but its meaning would be clear to the man who read it: I think you're wrong and I can say so where it matters. On your own head be it.

An hour later yet again and Rickoff was looking at a final message. The attempt was authorized: Rickoff had *carte blanche*. He smiled in a grim amusement. It was a matter of knowing the ropes. If he'd asked for *carte blanche* he'd never have been given it. Never in a hundred years.

Rickoff looked at the clock. He had wasted three hours but he had plenty of time to give orders still. His planning he had done in the intervals of signalling. It was fortunate that there was a warship quite so close—that was an excellent omen. The British were playing with a new submarine and the destroyer had been shadowing. Outside the limit, naturally, but the ship was a shell for a floating laboratory. She could easily put a launch ashore somewhere west of Portland. It would be three in the morning before the grey car reached the rendezvous and there wouldn't be a moon. Rickoff had already sent a warning message to the captain and now he sent confirmation. The captain was to pick his own spot and report it by half-past eleven at latest. The cars would start for Gilston Road at a quarter to twelve exactly.

Cars, Rickoff thought, not car. They'd need at least three. It would be absurdly optimistic to assume that his conversation with Starc hadn't been listened to. All the signs were that it had been. So what would the British know from it? Rickoff began to tick it off. They'd know where Starc was and Starc was a wanted man. Those idiot Poles had failed—he'd deal with that later—and a policeman had seen them failing. Every policeman in London would have been looking for Starc and now they would know he was at Gilston Road. Where he'd once had an assignment, the foolish fellow-traveller Margaret Palfrey. That explained why he had gone there but not why Gorjan had too. For the moment that didn't matter. There'd be plenty of time to interrogate Gorjan later.

What else would the British know? That Starc had telephoned to a man called Rickoff. That was bad but it wasn't disastrous. He had known for some time that he was suspect already and he wouldn't object to transfer. If he could pull off this evening's work and well, deliver up Gorjan alive, he could ask for what he fancied. And he'd get it.

But it wouldn't be easy since the British would know of two things more. They'd have heard Gorjan's name and they'd have heard the appointment at midnight. Gilston Road would be crawling with police and Executive. Rickoff grinned. A grey car, he'd said, at midnight.

They'd need more than one car, they would indeed. They'd have to make a run for it, and a three-hour journey was inconveniently long. It was possible there'd be shooting but he certainly wouldn't start it. Shooting made a gamble of the best-laid plans. Instead they'd have to run for it, and the grey job was faster than any known police car. Even so there was traffic, even at midnight, and traffic was unpredictable. The grey job mustn't be unprotected. So there'd be another crew behind it trained in blocking pursuit or ditching it. And the police would have more than one car out so he'd make it two himself: the escape car, *two* blocks. That made three cars.

Rickoff corrected himself. That made four cars, since he needed one for Starc. Starc would be going too, though he hadn't decided where.

Stevan Starc had passed the most exhausting day of his life. The need to keep three people under surveillance hadn't especially troubled him, for Gorjan was still insensible, Margaret was too frightened to do anything but what he told her, and Lee had behaved with a casual calm which had astonished him. But the mounting nervous tension had left him spent.

Happily there had been things to do, small decisions to take but vital. For instance the telephone. Margaret was frightened but she wasn't to be trusted, and there was a case for ripping the wire out. Stevan Starc dismissed it. Somebody might telephone and, finding the number unobtainable, report to the engineers. It would be foolish to court intrusions. That was the reason Starc gave himself but there was also another: Rickoff might ring him—put an end to his uncertainty. God knew they had business unfinished.

Starc put the thought behind him, finding a brief relief in the tasks which were now demanded. Margaret had bandaged Mellion Lee, but Starc could see she had done it clumsily and he did it again himself. He'd been within finger-pull of killing her but he'd shot to stop Lee, not hurt him. He'd aimed for the shoulder and got it. The bullet had gone in and out and no bone seemed broken. Lee had been lucky. He'd had a broken nose already and now he had a flesh wound; he had lost some blood but his condition wasn't dangerous. Starc could tell he was in pain but not intolerably. He tied the right arm in a sling. He had put away his pistol, for he hated waving firearms like some sheriff in a Western. Even threats had been unnecessary. In a fashion Starc wouldn't have wished to define Mellion Lee held the better hand. He knew it too. Lee wouldn't make trouble— he didn't need to. Mellion Lee was content to wait.

Stevan Starc wasn't. As the hours crawled away his nerves crawled with them. It hadn't been so bad at first but later it was unbearable. At first there had been Lee to fix and later they'd looked at Gorjan. He was still unconscious, breathing heavily and irregularly, and Starc had known that there was nothing they could do for him. Margaret Palfrey had once been a doctor, but he wouldn't have trusted her to treat Lee's nose, far less what he suspected was a serious injury to the brain. They had made Gorjan comfortable and left him, and later Lee had asked for food. Starc would have choked on it, but he had gone with them to the kitchen. Margaret had made coffee and

Starc had drunk it gratefully. But Lee wanted eggs and surprisingly had eaten three left-handed. Afterwards they had all gone back to the living-room.

By late afternoon Starc was as taut as a drumskin. He told himself grimly that he had reason to be so. For nothing had been settled—nothing about himself. Rickoff knew that Gorjan was there and Rickoff would send for him. That much was certain but nothing else. No bargain had been struck and none was possible. One didn't bargain with the Rickoffs, since a promise made was as frail as was the breath which bore it. One did them a favour—a duty they'd consider it—and hoped. An undreamt-of success might perhaps expunge a failure.

Or again it might not. That was something which a good communist must unquestioningly accept. Starc wasn't, this evening, feeling such a good communist.

He was suddenly conscious that Mellion Lee was smiling at him. Lee was sitting in an armchair much too small for him and Margaret was in another. Lee said unexpectedly: 'There's a drink if you want it.'

'No thank you.'

'You mean you don't dare.'

'You're observant,' Starc said.

'I don't need to be a psychiatrist to see that you're under strain.'

'Yes, I'm waiting.'

'Would it help if I talked then?'

Starc said reluctantly: 'It might.'

'I think it would. But we've only one subject in common.'

Lee began to talk politics, Starc listening in a kind of shame. For this man wasn't ignorant. Starc had been taught to think of all Americans as fools, as men who thought only of money and sometimes when they had made enough of it of the capitalist degeneracy called the arts. They were slaves to their women, sheep in sheep's clothing, and much too lazy mentally to bother with the realities of power. But Lee didn't think like that. He made none of the intellectual genuflections to communism which in Margaret Palfrey irritated Starc intolerably. He was an anticommunist but he gave excellent reasons to be so: communism would destroy him, his way of life and his private privileges; he didn't talk democracy, he talked about wealth; he had money and stood to lose it. Starc listened respectfully. They had told him the West was blind; it mouthed meaningless words but was incapable of thinking. But this man thought clearly. Starc disagreed but he couldn't despise, for this was a decent obverse to the medal he wore himself. And Lee wasn't unfair. The price of communism was appalling, its achievement, cost-accounted, more than a little commonplace, but certainly there had been achievement and without it there might have been none. Starc didn't dispute—he was learning. This man was wrong but he wasn't a pink liberal. And the emergent nations, the tiresome statelings which blurred the firm outlines of world politics? Nothing could be more admirable than communist treatment of them. Communism seldom gave handouts, above all it never bribed. Some tedious huddle of tribal Africans wished to reform itself? Then by all means let it. If it chose the road of communism it could be sure of complete protection: no wicked colonialism would be permitted to re-enslave it. But it must pull itself up by its own black bootstraps. Other communist states had done the same and God, how they'd suffered. Communism wasn't philanthropy. All this chatter about aid to the underdeveloped nations. Mellion Lee thought it misconceived.

Presently he looked again at Starc. 'I've been talking,' he said on a note of apology.

'I've been interested and I'm grateful. I wish I'd known you before. I wish I'd really *known* you.'

'Twice, wasn't it? and at parties. Diplomatic parties are a grave for time. I didn't recognize you when you first came in.'

'I know I don't look like a diplomat.' Starc heard himself laugh and it astonished him. 'You were much too polite to ask me questions.'

'You told me how you got in here.'

'Yes.' There was a silence, but unembarrassed. Neither man looked at Margaret Palfrey for both had forgotten her. It was a moment of reflection not of hate. Lee broke it at last.

'If I could ask you a question now. . . .'

'Go on.'

'Did you know Gorjan was here?'

'No, that was luck. Or I hope it was luck.'

'You haven't the air of hope, you know. I heard you use the telephone. Not what you said but I heard you use it.'

'And you've been thinking since?'

Lee began a shrug but stopped himself; he made a grimace, half-humorous, half of pain. Starc said: 'I'm sorry about your shoulder.'

'You could just as well have killed me. I thought you were a communist.'

'That doesn't make me a murderer—not pointlessly.'

'I can see I've got a lot to learn.' Mellion Lee was laughing too. 'You've taught me the same.'

There was another long silence, this time relaxed, almost the silence of friends. Stevan Starc said reflectively: 'So you heard me on the telephone. And what did you make of that?'

'Only the negative. You wouldn't have been telephoning to the police, nor yet to your own ambassador. Either would have been here by now.'

'You've a logical mind.'

'I was once a mathematician. Not a good one but I might have been.'

'But you went into diplomacy.'

'I went. And a diplomat knows that there's more than one sort of communist.'

'Then you guessed what I'm waiting for?'

Mellion Lee didn't answer; he went to a cupboard, prising the door open with his foot. 'I don't think a drink would hurt us now. Just one.'

'All right, I'll help you.'

Stevan Starc mixed the whisky and Margaret made a tiny noise. Both men looked surprised but neither apologized. Starc gave her a drink silently. When they were sitting down again he said: 'May I ask you a question in turn?'

'Of course.'

'I came here on the run because I'd nowhere to go. And what I find is Alexander Gorjan and an American diplomatist. He's Scientific Counsellor at his embassy and he tells me he was once a mathematician. I also find a case of drugs. And pentothal. I've heard of it.'

'As it happens I haven't used it. You can believe that or not.'

'If you say so I believe you. Not that it's important.'

'Why not?'

Stevan Starc said deliberately: 'Gorjan has been very ill. As far as I knew he was still in hospital. Yet he's here in this flat unconscious. I'm no sort of doctor but I should say his state was critical. Even without pentothal you're taking appalling risks.'

'I'd have taken him back to hospital.'

'But when?'

'When he'd answered my questions.'

'And if he'd died answering them?'

'I suppose I'd have swung on an English rope.'

Stevan Starc's smile was a little sad. Almost with regret he said: 'There's no difference between us.'

In Rickoff's world secrecy was a habit but it was also a disease. He hadn't even known that the East German was in London, but he was unquestionably his superior and when he had been sent for he had gone immediately. Now they were talking. The East German was a Prussian: his short bull neck and clipped grey hair proclaimed it with an indecent pride. He was that most dangerous of men, one who would work for any master provided he would allow him to use his talents. Which were accepted as considerable, even by Rickoff, who hated all Germans. He was saying now: 'Gorjan alive would be an unexpected coup.'

'If we can bring it off.'

'Quite so. Certain aspects of this matter puzzle me, but you tell me you have authority.'

'I have.'

'Does it cover this Stevan Starc?'

'No, nothing was said of Starc.'

'Then may I ask what you intend for him?'

Rickoff sighed softly. He was a dedicated man but he knew he had a weakness. It was a sense of fair play and he had always had to fight it. He said in a sort of self-excuse: 'We shouldn't have Gorjan without Starc's help.'

'How is that relevant? His orders were to kill him and he failed. Moreover his failure has compromised us all. The English will be on notice, the English *know*. And he knows much too much himself.'

'Yes, that is true.'

'Then there is only one course open to us.'

Rickoff said reflectively: 'To encourage the others?'

'I do not think that funny.'

'No, I suppose it's not.' Rickoff thought again. 'Here?' he asked finally.

'You can make it look like suicide?'

'I can. And the British authorities will have motive not to pry too much.'

'In the circumstances I quite see that. We are agreed, then?'

'I can do as you instruct.'

'*Sehr richtig,*' the Prussian said.

At eleven o'clock that evening Colonel Charles Russell began to check his dispositions in the area of Gilston Road. He had once read a detective story in which the head of Scotland Yard had disguised himself. With a hairy great false beard at that. Russell had been horrified and had thrown the book down angrily. He wasn't the head of Scotland Yard but the officer in question was a very good friend, and Russell knew that he would cheerfully have died before putting a false beard on. He himself was dressed for an evening's prowling. He wore a Raglan overcoat of unfashionable cut and a cloth cap full of fishing flies. This wasn't an affectation. The barbs had rusted and he couldn't get the flies out without ruining the cloth. And he was attached to that cap as he was to old friends generally. He was carrying an umbrella and was unarmed. Four paces behind him walked a younger man. He carried a walkie-talkie and something else.

Charles Russell looked around him for it wasn't an area he knew well. Once it had been fashionable and to the east it still was. Now it was fading into a sort of gentility. It would have been interesting to speculate but he hadn't the time. His interest was in Forty-four and he knew about that. There was the ex-Indian Civilian in the bottom flat, Margaret Palfrey's was the top, and the middle was unoccupied. Or rather it had been. Now Robert Mortimer had quietly installed himself. He had a radio too, and Russell beckoned his young man up.

'Get me Mortimer, please.'

The walkie-talkie buzzed, then Robert Mortimer came through.

'Mortimer here.'

'It's Russell. Checking.'

'Everything is in order, sir. I can see the road without being seen.'

'Good.' It was good but not essential, for Mortimer's first duty wasn't to watch for the grey car's arrival. Others would see it before him. There were men in the Fulham Road and more in the Boltons. None of them was noticeable for all of them were skilled. And all were on the radio net. Mortimer's chief task was different and Russell began to inquire of it.

'Can you see through the door of the flat?'

'I've cut a sort of spy hole.'

'That's important. We want notice how many are coming down. It will probably be only whoever goes in, plus, of course, Starc. They won't bother with Gorjan's body, but it would be awkward if Lee and Mrs Palfrey came out too. I don't see why they should but they'd be most unwelcome witnesses. That's why you're there—to hold Lee and Palfrey. Can you hear any movements above you?'

'No, this is a well-built house. But I can see through the door —the landing and some of the stairs. They'll have to come past me.'

'Good again. Keep awake.'

Russell passed back the walkie-talkie, resuming his rounds. The tape had spoken of a single car but Russell expected several. This was a snatch, comparable though more insolent, to throwing a brick through a jeweller's and decamping. And the best snatch-and-grab men always had a block car. Here there might be more than one for the run-out could be a long one. There wasn't a ship of Rickoff's flag anywhere in the River, and though there were some satellites it was Russell's hunch that Rickoff wouldn't risk them. In any case they were watched and could be stopped. Rickoff would guess that too. None of his aircraft was grounded at London Airport, and the same applied there; aircraft weren't hard to stop. So it looked like a run for some lonely beach and the objective was quite unknown. Yes, the run-out might be a long one for the block cars.

Except that they wouldn't start.

Russell walked on steadily, going first to a car in Tregunter Road. It looked like a Wolseley and some of it was. But not very much. This was the police car. It had a uniformed crew of three, and Russell noticed with approval that they were rather older than a normal crew. So they'd been picked for their discretion as he'd asked. In the back was a man in plain clothes whom Russell recognized. This man said pleasantly: 'I know it's your evening but I hope you'll forgive a gatecrash.'

'I'm enchanted to see you.'

Russell went on. His own car was in Harley Gardens and there was a reserve in Creswell Place. He checked the latter first, then his own, finally what looked like a taxi in the *cul de sac* of Milborne Grove. It looked like a taxi but there were interesting differences. The chief was the armour. The taxi wasn't armoured against gunfire, or not against gunfire primarily, but it could go into a head-on crash and the driver could walk away from it. Or it could take a car sideways and tear both the wheels off. The driver was smoking a quiet cigar and Russell went up to him.

'Is everything all right?'

James Scobell nodded.

'You like the new London taxis?'

'Sure. I've had time for a bit of practice too. I'm glad I once drove a Sherman. It was nice of you to cut me in.'

'You often cut *me* in.'

'Will you have a cigar?'

Russell looked at his watch. 'I don't think I'll waste a good cigar. Afterwards.'

'Okay.'

Russell returned to his own big car. There were two men in the front and Russell and the young man climbed in behind. Russell looked at his watch again. It was eleven-forty precisely so he still had twenty minutes. He said to his bodyguard: 'Wake me when the party starts.'

In two minutes he was peacefully asleep.

CHAPTER 17

At a few minutes to midnight the man beside Russell woke him. 'Their cars are coming down,' he said, 'they're in the Boltons now.'

'How many are there?'

'Four.'

Russell jumped out, striding briskly into Gilston Road, the young man still with him. Opposite Number Forty-four he halted, the width of the street between himself and the house. Four cars were driving down Gilston Road on sidelights only. They were spaced with the precision of a troop of tanks, coming from the north on Russell's side. But fifty yards short of him the driver of the leader put his hand out. The cavalcade swung smoothly across the road, stopping in front of Forty-four. Two men got out from the second car, climbing the seven steps. The front door had been unlocked and they went in.

Russell took the radio, flicking the switch to centralize. 'Acknowledge,' he said.

They began to come in in turn, the monitor at headquarters, the police car in Tregunter Road, Russell's own, the reserve in Creswell Place, James Scobell's taxi and finally Robert Mortimer. To the last Russell said: 'Any movement upstairs?'

'None that I can hear, but they've gone past me going up. Two men.'

'I saw.'

Russell began to cross the street. He handed the walkie-talkie to his bodyguard, but as they went across the road the young man gave it back again. 'If you wouldn't mind holding the box, sir.'

'Oh, I see.' Charles Russell took back the radio and the young man put his right hand in the pocket of his overcoat. Russell said calmly: 'I hope you won't have to use it. That would spoil everything.'

They walked side by side down the line of cars. There were three men in the first, a driver alone in the second, and the driver and one other man in each of the last two. They wore hats which by European standards were unfashionably large and they stared at Russell with curious hostile eyes. None of them spoke as he walked by inspecting them. When he had finished he returned to the opposite pavement, saying to the bodyguard: 'Counting the two men inside that's ten of them. They don't spare expense. Now what about the cars themselves?'

'The one opposite the steps is presumably the escape car. It's the new 300 Merc—fuel-injection and fast as hell. The two behind are identical but I don't recognize the make. The one in front with a three-man crew is a Ford Cortina. I don't know what it's doing here. Even if they've hotted her she couldn't live with the Merc or us.'

'Not a pilot, then?'

'It couldn't be.'

'A decoy perhaps?'

'Perhaps.'

'We'll leave it for now but we'd better begin the party.' Russell returned to the radio, speaking to the police car. 'Come into Gilston Road. Stay on the east side, the same side I am, but stop twenty yards north of me. Face south and keep the engine on. . . . Harley Gardens? There are four of their cars, all pointing at Fulham Road, but we don't want a break-back. Prevent it.'

Half a minute later Gilston Road had been blocked where the twin curves of the Boltons joined it. The radio said: 'In position, sir.'

'Good. . . . Milborne Grove?'

James Scobell answered and Russell went on. 'There are a couple of block cars. Repeat, a couple. We don't know the make but they've left fifteen yards between them.'

'That's very considerate.' The fine western whine was entirely cool.

'I see what you mean. Come up to the corner but stay in Milborne Grove. . . . Mortimer?'

'Voices, I think, but no movement yet. . . . Wait. I heard a door open.'

Russell spoke again to James Scobell. 'It's time for your bit of fun. Don't miss.'

A taxi came round the corner from Milborne Grove, changing gear quickly but not into top, accelerating surprisingly. It was driving along the right-hand side but just short of the block cars it swerved. It took the first on a calculated curve, tearing at its nearside wheel, leaving it crumpled uselessly. The impact had barely checked the taxi's run. The driver pulled slightly out, a yard perhaps, then banged his left hand down, taking the second block car almost square, crushing its radiator into an untidy concertina. There was a shocking sound of outraged steel, a good deal of steam and swearing. The taxi began to back. All its mudguards seemed to have fallen off and they lay in the road neglected. What had been below them glinted dully in the street lamps. The taxi completed its deliberate back, then drove away steadily. The growl of its diesel faded, then was gone.

Four men had climbed from the two wrecked cars, standing on the pavement uncertainly. Other men had appeared from nowhere. They didn't interfere; they stood. There were many more than four of them. Flashlights popped alarmingly and the four foreigners threw their arms up much too late. They swore again but they didn't move. The men in the front two cars had not got out. They too were covered now.

Charles Russell crossed the road again, picking his way between the ruins of the block cars. At the foot of the steps of Forty-four he spoke again to Mortimer: 'Anything moving?'

'No. . . . Yes. They're coming downstairs.' A moment of silence, then, incredulously: 'They've got Gorjan.'

'You mean they're bringing his body out?'

'That's what it looks like.' Another small silence, this time of uncertainty. 'They've each got an arm round his shoulders. It isn't the way you carry a stiff. His head's lolling down, but it's sort of moving. I——'

Russell said peremptorily: 'Mortimer, make your mind up.'

'His legs are trailing. . . . No. He's more than half out but he isn't dead.' Mortimer's voice went up a tone. *'Gorjan's alive.'*

It was the last news he'd expected but Russell accepted it instantly. He said: 'Henderson, come here,' and a man in a raincoat detached himself from the others. He stood silently on Russell's left, the bodyguard on his right. Russell had put the walkie-talkie on the pavement. The three men stood, at the bottom of the steps but clear of them. They waited.

The front door opened and a spotlight flamed blindingly. A man held Gorjan on either side. They blinked in the unexpected glare, hesitatingly, talking softly. Then they came down the steps collectedly. The trio at the bottom didn't move.

On the last step but one the others halted. They could see a little now. There was a semi-circle of silent faces watching them, a cloth-capped man in an ancient overcoat solidly at its centre. He was carrying an umbrella still but unmistakably he commanded. The cars were quite cut off.

Very faintly Gorjan groaned. He had opened his eyes.

The cloth-capped man said formally: 'This *is* a surprise. A pleasant one.'

The man on Gorjan's right had his left arm round his shoulders. His right was free and now he began to move it.

'I wouldn't.' On Russell's right the bodyguard had a gun out.

The other saw it and dropped his hand. He stared at Charles Russell, still holding Gorjan, then, half in resignation, half in rage, he pushed Gorjan at him. Gorjan swung over on useless legs, all but falling finally. Russell staggered but held him. The man on the step said in excellent English: 'I'm a diplomat. I've immunity.'

'The former is alas correct, the latter exaggerates wildly.'

'So? But you'd be wise to forget this little farce.'

'Oddly enough I mean to.' Russell spoke to the man in a raincoat. 'Put them both in the Mercedes, the four from the block cars too. And photograph those you haven't already taken. Then let them go. Detain the small car in front, with crew.'

Stevan Starc had appeared in the doorway. The spotlight was off but somebody turned it on again. Russell said crossly: 'Turn that damned thing off.' They took Gorjan from him and he walked up the steps.

Seven steps, seven seconds. It was enough for another decision.

'Monsieur Stevan Starc?'

Stevan Starc nodded.

'This isn't quite what I expected. I'd expected Gorjan dead. After all you tried to kill him once.'

'Those two men talked?'

'They did.'

Starc said indifferently: 'They always talk in time.'

'Why didn't you kill Gorjan in there?'

Starc didn't answer.

'Then I don't think you can blame me if I draw my own conclusion. Which is that he was more valuable to you alive. To you, monsieur, personally.'

'Perhaps I had hoped so.'

'There's a fourth car here which puzzled me. There are or were a car for Gorjan, two block cars, and a fourth. The fourth is still here and the crew's still with it.'

'Four cars,' Starc said thoughtfully.

'Four cars.'

'Then there might have been one for me.'

Russell said levelly: 'Not might have been—it is.'

'But I haven't got Gorjan.'

'I know.'

'How long can you get in England for attempted murder?'

'I don't want you publicly tried.'

'Then something less orthodox suits you?'

Charles Russell nodded.

There was a silence which Starc broke at last; he said in a calm flat voice: 'Then we'd better walk down to that other car.'

They went together to the Cortina. There was a seat in front empty, and Starc climbed in. For a second Russell hesitated. This was an enemy but it was also a brave man. . . . Power grows out of the end of a gun. That wasn't a dictum popular with humanists but that didn't make it contemptible. Russell raised his hand in what was almost a salute.

'Goodbye,' he said.

As the car drove away he heard Starc laugh.

CHAPTER 18

The news of Starc's death was in both Russell's papers next morning, handled discreetly in one, mercilessly splashed in the other. He read without surprise and without too much attention, for there would be a full report on his desk at the Executive.

An hour later he was reading it. Starc had been found on Barnes Common dead and clearly it was suicide. He had shot himself through the mouth, upwards into the brain, and the gun had been lying with him. There were the powder burns of a self-inflicted injury and finger prints on the pistol. They had been Starc's and there hadn't been others.

Charles Russell put the report away. Later in the morning a senior policeman in plain clothes would call on him. He'd know what had happened in Gilston Road; he'd know because he'd been there. He wouldn't ask for instructions but he'd sound Russell delicately on the Executive's intentions. . . . Finding Gorjan alive had obviously changed the basis of an evening's entertainment. Starc had driven away without pursuit, which could only have happened if Russell had allowed it. No doubt he had had good reasons in the surprisingly altered circumstances, and the motives which moved the Executive weren't matters for the police unless they had to be. Which was not the case here. Three men had driven away with Starc, but there wasn't a shred of evidence to connect them with Barnes Common, nothing you could put before a court. In any case Starc was a diplomat who was known to have been in trouble—private trouble; he had in fact been on the run. It looked like suicide, and an inquest would certainly find so if it wasn't encouraged not to. That suited Colonel Russell? Then it suited the police too.

And Starc's own ambassador was putting out a story which supported a simple suicide. The Press was besieging Nikola Mitrovic but he was handling it skilfully. He was much too experienced to refuse to talk at all. That would have been suspicious and therefore fatal. Instead he was hinting at women and money, giving them half a story. The populars would run it hard, then, after the inquest, kill it. The police hadn't found the Poles who had tried to kill Starc, so there was no need to link that aspect with Starc's suicide. They didn't think they'd ever find them now—almost certainly the men were out of England. And the three foreigners who had driven away with Starc, the other hoodlums of Gilston Road—presumably the Executive would prefer to deal with that side.

The senior policeman's presumption would be correct. Russell would accept responsibility for any foreigner seen and flash-photographed in Gilston Road and he'd accept it very willingly. It was the first of all charges on the Security Executive that it avoid international embarrassments and Russell had planned deliberately to do so. Ten photographs would discreetly find their way on to a certain official's desk and, since the rules were agreed by both sides when they were mutually of advantage, the faces on the photographs would quietly disappear. Of course they'd be promptly replaced: Russell couldn't stop it and he wasn't sure he wanted to. This was an open society and he'd accepted its terms of service. The price of it too. That was something which a security officer did well to remember. One who did not was soon a menace.

Charles Russell frowned. He had experience to guide him in dealing with chauffeurs to an embassy who did more things than drive motor cars, but Lee and Mrs Palfrey raised an unaccustomed problem. They were coming to see him that afternoon—the invitation had been courteous but unmistakably an instruction—and he didn't know what to say to them. He corrected himself for that wasn't right; he knew what to say, he had plenty of cards, but he wasn't quite sure how to play them. Starc had had orders to kill Gorjan; he had known what that meant and he'd paid the price of failure. Halted before his Maker, Russell would have admitted to a certain admiration for Stevan Starc. But Lee had been less forthright and in Russell's view more criminal. Drugs had been found at Forty-four, though there hadn't been time to use them. But the intention had been established, there had been violence on a man in convalescence, then a dangerously sick one had been ruthlessly kept from hospital. They wouldn't know all the details till Gorjan had fully recovered and could talk. And it looked as though he would. The bulletin from the Hemmingway was hopeful. They'd decided they'd have to operate, but Gorjan was a hard one, strong as the splendid oxen which worked his own country's fields. So with luck he'd recover but not thanks to Lee. Lee was a friend in name, a guest, and he'd grossly abused another. A sick one at that. Inviting him to a neutral house, putting him to the Question. . . .

Mellion Lee and Stevan Starc—Russell had no doubt which he preferred. And now Starc had been found on Barnes Common dead, the victim of a suicide which Russell knew well was not. But Lee was a friendly diplomat so they'd never let Russell nail him. Lee would go free and that wasn't just.

Russell reined himself sharply. A security officer who didn't accept the terms of the society which employed him was a menace, but there was one sort more dangerous. It was the security officer who indulged in moral judgements. The first was a poor official and that was bad: the second was worse because merely ridiculous. Just the same one had a conscience and Mellion Lee outraged it. Starc stiff on a Common, Lee walking away scot free. . . .

Well, perhaps not quite freely. Charles Russell smiled unamiably. Perhaps not quite freely. There was also Margaret Palfrey and there were possibilities in Margaret. That was why he had sent for them both.

They were shown in at tea-time though Russell didn't offer it. He put them opposite his desk. Lee was wearing a clean arm sling and his nose was in plaster. Russell stared at them coldly. He had a level blue eye and his stare could be disconcerting. Ordinarily he never stared, for he was a considerate man and detested anything savouring of one-upmanship. But this afternoon he stared them both down deliberately. Margaret's eyes dropped first but Lee took a little longer. With an untypical formality Russell said: 'Both of you have caused me too much trouble.'

They neither answered.

'Moreover you're still an embarrassment. You, Mr. Lee—I loathe what you've done with all my heart, but that's a sub-jective judgement and you're entitled to ignore it. What embarrasses me is that you chose to act in England. And madam—yourself. I'm prepared to believe that you're an accessory at worst but the fact remains that apart from what you may have done you've both of you seen too much.'

Mellion Lee said thoughtfully: 'Such as this morning's newspapers?'

'And certain events last night. So far they haven't been con-nected with a death on Barnes Common. I prefer it that way.'

'You're frightened we'll talk?' Lee asked. He didn't himself sound frightened.

'Your father owns newspapers.'

'I don't think he'd use them to break a son's career.'

Russell nodded approvingly. 'A good debating point.' He turned to Margaret Palfrey. 'And you?'

'I wouldn't hurt Mellion either.'

'And how can I be sure of it? You're not man and wife.'

Mellion Lee looked up sharply but Russell went on. He had always found it difficult to sustain the formal manner and now he relapsed into workaday Russell. 'Look at it from my seat. I've excellent strings on both of you but they're separate strings. You follow me?'

Lee shook his head.

'I'd have thought it was obvious.' Charles Russell was being patient. 'Mr Lee I could jail on a choice of charges and if any-one talked I'd have to. *And that's just what I'm afraid of.* Mrs Palfrey is less vulnerable personally, but she'd certainly be in it deep if there were any sort of publicity. When of course she might talk to save her skin.'

'I'll never do that.'

'I've heard this before but how can I be sure of it?'

Mellion Lee said slowly: 'What are you getting at?'

'You force me to state what I'd hoped you'd gather. I'd like to see you married.'

'*Married?*'

'Of course. Then instead of a string on each of you I'd have one on a married couple. Who'd each have a string on the other. Simplicity is a rule of my profession.'

Surprisingly Lee laughed but Margaret didn't; she began to protest but Russell stopped her; from a drawer in his desk he produced a passport. 'Yours,' he said blandly. 'Yours again in three weeks, or much less if you know the right people.' His voice changed to quotes. ' "But a special licence is granted by the Archbishop of Canterbury, under special circumstances, for marriage at any place, with or without previous residence in the district, or at any time et cetera; but the reasons assigned must meet with His Grace's approval." . . . Do you happen to know His Grace?'

'I dare say I could get at him.'

'Not the happiest of phrases.'

But Mellion Lee was no longer laughing; pointing at Margaret's passport he said coldly: 'Have you stolen mine too?'

'As it happens I haven't. But it's in very good hands.'

'Whose hands?'

'I must call it a trade secret.'

'But I could always get another.'

'You're very welcome to try.'

'So you've fixed things with my embassy as well?'

'Let's say they've been fixed.'

'By whom?'

'By a friend of some influence. We've an interest in common, which is to kill this story finally.'

With an astonishing lack of venom Mellion said: 'But this is blackmail.'

'Yes.'

'You're a no-good high-up criminal.'

'Yes.'

'I suppose I ought to hit you.'

'No.'

Mellion Lee had risen suddenly but not to strike Russell. He took Margaret's arm and pulled her up. 'Come on—talking's over.' He pushed her through the door and turned himself. To Russell he said: 'Goodbye.'

'I very sincerely hope so.'

Russell had risen too. He poured himself the sherry which he kept for occasions of merit. Starc had been found on a Common dead but Mellion Lee was lumbered. That was satisfying —justice. Russell drank his own health. Careless for once of syntax he said happily: 'That'll learn 'em.'

Mellion Lee took Margaret to an unpretentious restaurant. He ordered quickly without consulting her. She wasn't offended; she preferred him like that. Presently he said casually: 'After we've eaten we'll apply for a licence.'

'You mean you'll give in to that wicked old man?'

'I wouldn't put it like that. Maybe Russell didn't put all his cards down; maybe he's even smarter than he seems.' Lee's smile was a boy's wide grin, gayer than she'd ever seen him. 'Maybe we deserve each other.'

'That isn't a compliment.'

'None was intended. But you're not a bad bitch as bitches go.'

She said angrily: 'So you'd marry me to keep your job.'

'Christ, I would not! I quit on my job three hours ago. Resigned.'

'You didn't tell Russell that.'

'Why the hell should I? He had a handful of aces whatever I told him.'

She thought out the implications. 'Then what are you going to do?'

'It's too late to go back to arithmetic, so I thought I might buy a newspaper. I'd run it against one of father's. I'd perhaps make him buy me out. You might even be mildly useful. You write terrible crap for some terrible papers but at bottom you're a journalist. Look at that piece on Alex Gorjan: it was quite first-class in its offbeat way. . . . Yes, I think I'll buy a newspaper. I'll make father sweat for once.'

'That would appeal to you?'

'It's a fair second best. Real work might save both of us.'

She said intensely: 'Mellion——'

He laughed at her. 'Real work, I said. I'm forty-five.'

The chief physician of the Hemmingway Hospital was purring contentedly. It had always been his opinion that Gorjan's illness was basically spino-neural, and now the eminent specialist from Zürich had confirmed his diagnosis. He had brushed the psychiatrist aside contemptuously. They weren't colleagues on the staff of the same hospital, and the Herr Doktor hadn't troubled to conceal his poor opinion. With the physician alone he had permitted himself an aside, something about a superstitious Austrian peasant. It hadn't been clear whether he was referring to the senior psychiatrist of the Hemmingway or whether he had had in mind a rather better known figure also of Austrian origin and the same profession. Not that the Swiss had allowed the word when the physician had used it. Profession! Fiddlesticks. What sort of a science was it which couldn't be verified by any means known to science, where controls were unknown, where the same experiment seldom produced the same result, and which claimed as the final absurdity that only its own initiates could judge it? A very German-Swiss snort had been balm to the Scot. And the Herr Doktor would be pleased to operate, there was really an excellent chance, and no, he need send for no assistance. There had been a polite little bow. If so eminent a colleague would be so obliging as to co-operate the Herr Doktor would be honoured.

Now the physician went upstairs to Gorjan's room. He was conscious but was heavily sedated. The physician checked him carefully and left.

Alexander Gorjan was heavily sedated but his mind had been working clearly. He knew they were going to operate and the doctors had told him there was no risk. He hadn't believed them, doctors always said that, but he had talked to Nikola Mitrovic. Nikola had hummed and hedged but finally he'd spoken. The odds, he'd been told, were on the right side of evens. Alex Gorjan had been content. He'd had a very good life and he'd lived every second of it. There had been plenty of occasions when the odds had been rather worse. That experiment two years ago, or the crash in the Maserati. He'd walked alive from both of them and he'd walk from this hospital too. He'd walk—they wouldn't carry him.

He slept for two hours, waking almost normal. The black nurse had come back and that was fine. There'd be convalescence no doubt, and that was fine too. Two or three months perhaps. Gorjan was far from dreading them. England was the perfect place for an important man who didn't feel self-important. If he had to stay abroad a while this arrogant considerate people would be his choice. And there'd be wine when he was well again, to civilize this sunless land, and books. Third but not least was this delicious blackamoor.

He took a hand from the sheets and waved at her. 'Hullo.'

'Oh, hullo.'

'I'm back again.'

'That's good.'

'Should a nurse say good when a patient gets wheeled in again?'

She showed magnificent teeth. 'I wouldn't know.'

'I hear they're going to cut me up.'

'That's nothing.'

'A nurse must say that,' he said.

'This one knows you're a very strong man. Oh, yes.'

'I shall be in a week or two.'

'I'm here on a six months' contract. Go to sleep.'

Nikola Mitrovic was concluding his interview with Gabriel Palliser. 'So,' he was saying, 'you see how it is. You know already why we sent Gorjan here, and I'm telling you we don't dare send him back yet. Equally we can't have him kicking his heels here without a reason—not after he's well again. Newspapers are too curious and most of your own too smart. So we're making a proposition. The essence, as I've just explained, is that he can work for you. He can work for you on anything but the interception of missiles by interfering with their guidance systems. I'm offering you eighty per cent of the best microwave man alive.'

'And how do we pay for it?'

'Simple. You keep him alive.'

'For how long do we have him?'

'I wish I knew that myself. I can't conceal that if developments go against us it might well be for some time.'

Palliser said thoughtfully: 'Of course the public story will be quite false. Gorjan asking for political asylum. . . .'

'Of course. It's not something I'd propose to every British Minister. That is a compliment.'

'I'm rather afraid it is.' The Minister reflected again. 'I'll have to talk to the P.M.,' he said.

'Pick one of his good days, please.'

His Excellency went out and, half an hour later, Palliser was talking to Charles Russell. The Minister had a nice taste in political irony and Mitrovic's proposal tickled it. Your enemies tried to kill a man, your allies to exploit him. Both of them failed. So the second-rate British were invoked to hold him safely. Palliser hadn't taken Mitrovic entirely seriously but nor had he dismissed the possibilities. Even retaining Gorjan in England would be something with a certain oblique prestige. It would be a card which could be played against the more aggressive diplomatic systems of friend and enemy alike. Palliser loved neither.

He explained to Russell what Mitrovic had proposed to him. Russell didn't interrupt. Palliser wasn't pompous, but even a good Minister didn't take kindly to hearing that an official already knew. From time to time Russell looked surprised but he held his experienced tongue. When he had finished Palliser asked: 'Do you think you could keep him safe?'

'I could try very hard. I would.'

'Then I'm tempted to let him stay. The working for us isn't on.'

'But it's got to be on. It's all or nothing.'

'Why?'

'Gorjan's not a man to stay anywhere doing nothing.'

'I hadn't thought of that side.' The Minister thought of it. 'Suppose,' he said, 'suppose——'

'There's the Advisory Council on Scientific Policy, there's A.E.A., there's the Department of Scientific and Industrial Research, there's——'

'If you were a first-class scientist, I mean first-class, would you be happy in any of those?'

'Frankly, I doubt it.'

'And so do I. On the other hand there's Sir William Banner. Bill Banner is an industrialist, a tycoon I suppose you'd call him, and he's always beefing that second- and third-class scientists are nine for sixpence. He'd do anything for a top-flight man and there's something I could ask him in return.'

'Yes?' The question was unnecessary—Russell didn't expect an answer. The monosyllable had been an expression of distaste. The Government would fall in months and Palliser would be jobless.

The Minister offered a cigarette from the case Russell deprecated. 'Suppose Gorjan went to Banner, what would Banner put him on to?'

'He's a microwave man so presumably on to microwaves. Did you know that our least successful airline was experimenting with microwave ovens which can reheat meals in a minute? Which is a twentieth of the time it now takes. But the microwave oven can't yet cope with as many meals as the traditional apparatus, and it interferes with an aircraft's electronics and radar systems. When those problems are solved catering on international flights is going to be a whole lot easier.'

Palliser said admiringly: 'The things you know. Where did you pick up that one?'

'I'll give you no guesses. I read it in *The Financial Times*.'

'My favourite newspaper. But I doubt if Bill Banner is heavily stuck in on microwave cooking. He's committed to plenty else, though. Plenty. Gorjan——'

Russell said sharply: 'There's a condition, you know—eighty per cent of him. We mustn't cheat.' He was remembering Nikola Mitrovic: 'You're a deceptively tough people and as crooked as they come. The only way to hold you is a gentleman's agreement.'

If the animal were extant still.

Russell repeated firmly: 'We mustn't cheat.'

The Minister looked at him with an expression Russell knew and loathed. He would have called it a politician's expression. Palliser broke it with a practised laugh. 'We mustn't,' he said coolly, 'be caught out cheating.'

Other SIGNET Thrillers You'll Enjoy

CALL FOR THE DEAD *by John Le Carré*
A canny British secret agent copes with an unusual case of espionage and murder. By the author of the superlative bestseller, *The Spy Who Came in from the Cold.*   (#D2495—50¢)

YOU ONLY LIVE TWICE *by Ian Fleming*
This bestselling James Bond adventure, set in Japan, is the twelfth addition to the Signet list of novels by the late Ian Fleming. Fleming's unique travelogue, *Thrilling Cities,* also appears in a Signet edition.   (#P2712—60¢)

INSPECTOR MAIGRET AND THE STRANGLED STRIPPER *by Georges Simenon*
The famous Inspector Maigret in the Paris underworld of prostitutes, addicts, and killers. Two additional Maigret mysteries are published in Signet editions, along with Simenon's recent bestseller, *The Bells of Bicêtre.*   (#D2580—50¢)

DAY OF THE GUNS *by Mickey Spillane*
Introducing a new kind of Spillane hero—Tiger Mann—a super-counter-espionage agent working to rout a Communist conspiracy at the United Nations.   (#D2643—50¢)

A MURDER OF QUALITY *by John Le Carré*
Ex-espionage agent George Smiley, hero of *Call for the Dead,* investigates a scandalous murder at one of England's famous public schools.
(#D2529—50¢)

NERVE *by Dick Francis*
Unexplained suicides baffle the steeplechase set in this thunderingly vital suspense novel set in England.   (#P2607—60¢)

PURSUIT (The Chase) *by Richard Unekis*
A canny police superintendent matches wits against two desperate fugitives who have committed what looks like the "perfect crime."   (#D2466—50¢)